About the author

Al Brookes lives in Brighton with her two dogs, who are small but robust. She has been a freelance writer for many years; this is her first novel.

To find out more about the author or give her some feedback, please visit www.albrookes.co.uk or email al@albrookes.co.uk

the GIFT *of* LOOKING CLOSELY

By Al Brookes

AB

First published in 2014 by
Al Brookes
Contact: al@albrookes.co.uk
Web: www.albrookes.co.uk

This book is a work of fiction.
Any resemblance to actual events, places or people,
living or dead, is entirely coincidental.

ISBN: 978-0-9928198-1-1

Acknowledgements

I am grateful to everyone who has supported me in getting this book out onto the pages, and especially to –

My writing family: Adam Pirani, Carol Bullock, Dave Nwokedi, Justine Kilkerr, Neela Masani, Russell McAlpine and Suzanne Donovan – they are talented writers and constructive critics (and wonderful companions on the quest to sample every type of flavoured vodka).

Morgan Marshall and *Karen Meador*, who were amazing first readers, enthusiastic and encouraging from the earliest draft.

Sam Duncan, who took the remarkable photograph on the front cover.

*E*ven now, I can feel myself disappearing.

 There was a time when I checked every day, studied the pale skin inside my wrists and elbows, imagined the flesh of my arms turned transparent, the blue veins running clear. Years later, I know the disappearing is more subtle than that, but I can't stop it. Not by myself.

 If just one person really knew me, I think it would be enough. One person who knew I have strange thoughts; that I see things I shouldn't; that my feelings bend me double.

 It's a lot to ask, especially now, when things are so intimate, so complex. But we won't start here, we'll go back to the beginning. There will be notes to fill in the gaps.

 You be Claire then, and I'll watch.

———

This is where you live:

 Down a short lane past the big houses on the left.

 Past green fields on the right.

 At the end of the lane, next to a churchyard without a church.

 This is where you've always lived, in the square white house with the grey slate roof. It was the vicar's house – there used to be a sign by the door – but your mother took it down the day they moved in; she said it wasn't the vicar's house anymore it was hers.

Two hundred years ago, the villagers took the church apart, piece by piece, used the bricks and windows to build something else. But even without the church, this is still consecrated ground. People are still buried under the gravestones.

As a child, you sat here in the summer, in the long grass with your back resting against James Frank Strong *you remember this still, feel the rough stone at your back, your shoulder blades tingling* while small lizards clattered along the boundary wall. On hot days you used a watering can to fill the stone birdbath and the orange lichen looked dry even when it was wet.

Sometimes you sat in the shade of the yew tree that had grown next to the church for a hundred years, then next to the church-shaped space left behind, shading the flagstones of the old church floor. You knew all the inscriptions on the gravestones. You still know most of them.

> Henry, son of George and Sarah Drake.
> February 25th 1848 aged 5 months
> Suffer little children to come unto me

> Also the above named George Drake.
> Died May 14th 1870 aged 54 years

> Also Sarah, widow of the above named Henry Drake
> Died July 12th 1882 aged 70 years

There are seventeen graves like this – the child buried first, the father, then the mother. The babies waited in the ground while their parents lived on.

In winter, you sat on the bench shaped like a cloverleaf, with three seats. You sat on a different seat each time *it had to be a different one each time – you left a sign to make sure you remembered, a chip of gravel or twigs placed one across another* with your feet tucked up. Sometimes, there were fox tracks in the snow.

There's a wooden gate, to the side, and a path from the churchyard into your own garden next door. Not a tended garden, a tangle. Bramble, ferns and wildflowers, always green because of the stream running along the back boundary and a tangle because that's how your mother liked it.

—

Your parents took out life insurance the day they got married. They couldn't imagine being able to breathe without each other, she said; let alone earn a living. You picture the way it happened. See:

> *Your parents – just married – in a bland office, a financial advisor's office. She sits on your father's lap, winds herself around him, smiles over his shoulder at the man in the suit behind the desk.*
>
> *'We can't breathe without each other,' she says.*

But when she died, he didn't stay off work for long; he couldn't bear to be at home without her and went back to his job within days, back to his library and his books. At home in the evenings, he spent hours sitting at the kitchen table, staring into space. He was too thin, his hair too long. You avoided him at first, stayed out as late as you could, working at the nursery until the sun went down. But once you realised that there would be no discussion, it wasn't so bad. You could sit for a long time together saying nothing. And then, finally, he would stand up.

'Time for bed, then.'

'Night, Dad.'

'Night, Claire.'

And you listened to his footsteps creaking on the stairs, passing over you along the narrow hallway to his bedroom. Their bedroom.

When the local library closed, he asked for a transfer. He

gave up on the house altogether, put it in your name and went to live in a flat in town by the sea. He calls now and then, asks how you are. He invites you to visit. It's been four years since you went.

—

This is what home means:

A dwelling place or fixed residence. An institution of refuge or rest.

From outside, your home is blank-faced, but it has its rules. You have to step down as you go through the front door into the kitchen. You have to duck your head going from the kitchen into the tiny living room. You have to turn sideways on the narrow staircase that leads down to the cellar. And when you go upstairs to the bedrooms, you have to step on a creaky stair because there are three creaky ones in a row and they are too steep to step over all at once.

Some of the rooms are more yours than others. The kitchen is yours, the round table almost entirely covered with your collected stuff – wood, small branches and twigs. Pebbles, snail shells, seed pods. They are clustered in vases and jam jars, packed into baskets. Every now and again, you look through each collection, taking stock, sorting. If you can no longer see the shapes that first captured your interest, you put them out in the garden or take them to the woods. You leave small bundles to fall apart gently in their own time, to decay unwatched.

So. The kitchen is yours, and the living room too. A small room, low-ceilinged, with one enormous striped sofa in front of the open fireplace, a coffee table, no room for anything else. Your gardening books and magazines are stacked under the table and next to the sofa. Left of the fireplace, there's a narrow wooden door painted the same cream as the walls; that's the door to the staircase.

Upstairs, the first bedroom is yours. There's a large bed in a small room *all those shameful bags and packages stuffed under the bed but you try not to think about them* with cream walls and cream bedding, and the same wild flower curtains you had when you were fourteen, the names in calligraphy. Foxglove. Cowslip. Loosestrife.

The bathroom is yours. One toothbrush. One towel.

The other bedroom, the one where your mother died, is still hers. And the study, in the extension off the back of the kitchen, still belongs to your parents, the two of them together.

—

This is where you keep your mother's letters:

In the study, in the writing bureau. In a dark wooden box the size of a shoebox, the lid inlaid with mother of pearl.

Inside, there are twenty-three letters written on thick cream paper. Your father gave them to you, wrapped in one of her silk scarves, the day after the funeral.

'Your mother left these for you,' he said, his eyes red-rimmed and flat. 'She started writing them as soon as she knew.' You looked down, began to count the worn stitches in the patterned carpet. When you looked up again, he was still offering the bundle, so you took it from him.

'She thought it might be a way to stay with you, even after she was gone,' he said.

You felt something then. Starting at the notch in your collarbone, it crept up into your throat. Nasty. You clamped your mouth shut and looked down again, until you heard your father's slippers pat a slow retreat.

You went to your room, carefully unwrapped the scarf. One by one, you unpeeled each envelope, read every letter very slowly, every word. There was no explanation. No apology. You put the letters away and didn't look at them again for a long time.

—

This is how it is when you wake up:

In the seconds between sleep and waking, you rise to the surface, dragging the weight of your dreams behind you. They are dreams of underwater creatures, pale and blind. You wish you could bend your sleeping thoughts into kinder shapes, create a place where the poor things could thrive. Instead you watch their slow progress through the murky water, concerned for their softness, fearful of eels with fins like razors hiding in the mud.

In the seconds between sleep and waking, you rise, squirming.

Some mornings, you open your eyes and let the feelings go. Some mornings, you can't. You lie in bed, watching the light filter through the curtains, while fear floats in the room. You are familiar with the way it works, this fear. It hovers, looking for something to attach to.

The dictionary is reassuring. In the dictionary, fear is just *a painful emotion caused by the presence of danger*; it can be pinned down by small black letters in short lines. In the dictionary, fear is put in its place, after *fealty*; given no more space or significance than *feather* or *feast*. It is pressed between hard covers.

You press your fear between the hard edges of real things – knotting the belt of your dressing gown; turning the head of the tap; cupping the flow of water in your palm until it warms. You pin it down with small actions – cutting a slice of bread; rinsing a plate; ironing a shirt.

In this way, by the time you step out of the house and pull the door shut behind you, you have made it small enough to take with you.

———

See. These are not comfortable shoes. But where they rub, where they hurt and most make you notice they aren't yours – those are the best places to get to know me. And it might get easier.

———

Now you're driving to work.

The road must have been warm when it rained; there's a thin steam hovering over the tarmac. The puddles reflect the blue-white sky, like milk. You are on a milky road between the hedges and shoulders of washed-clean fields. There are no other cars. The road unfurls. Water whispers under your tyres.

You change gear automatically at the last bend, where the trees create a tunnel of new leaves above you. The diesel engine is louder than ever; there is a hole in the exhaust. You change down again to turn right into the gravel parking area. The small stones crunch and rub under your boots as you get out. When you first came here, to earn some pocket money and learn about growing things, the gravel used to chatter under your sandals.

Little has changed since then. The two massive greenhouses that were so new when you first arrived have weathered, and the shop and the house both need painting. But the plants are still arranged the same way, grouped in alphabetical order. Perennials A to Z. Shade-loving plants and alpines. Shrubs and roses. Climbers and trees at the far end.

You can stand anywhere in the nursery and turn three hundred and sixty degrees without seeing another building, just a soft horizon in different shades of green. You wonder how much of the adjoining land Mr Holub actually owns. He has never mentioned it, but it seems strangely lucky that none of the neighbouring fields have been developed in all these years.

Matti is here today. Martin's nephew. He runs out on chubby legs to say hello, wants to help you in the greenhouse.

———

You cup the seeds in your hand so Matti can see them. He places the tip of one finger into the centre of your palm.

'They look like bugs.'

You think so too. Tiny black beetles that could unfold hidden legs and walk away if they chose. Nigella seeds are special.

Sooty and solid.

'Look. This is what they came out of,' you say.

Matti takes the round dry seedpod from you, holds its stem carefully between finger and thumb.

'It's a puffer! We saw one at the quarium. It holds its breath and gets fat and its prickles stick out.'

He shakes the pod, making the seeds rattle.

'I've woken them up – they want to get out!'

> I'm not so sure, little boy. Nice safe pod. Why would they want to leave?

You lift him onto a stool in front of the potting table and set him to work filling a seed tray with compost. He makes it an act of concentration, working in careful handfuls, while you quickly fill and level two dozen more and line them up along the bench.

'Sprinkle the seeds all over, Matti,' you say. 'It's okay to use too many. When they come up, we'll pull some of them out.'

He looks worried. 'Can't we let all of them grow?'

'They won't have room. We have to give the stronger ones the space they need.'

You sound so sensible, so efficient. But you don't like doing it either.

'What will the flowers be like, Auntie Claire?'

Clear and blue, you tell him. Flowers that look like they're made of paper. You tell him their common name: Love-in-a-Mist. Then he wants to know why they're called that.

'I guess because the leaves are very fine – the petals look like they're surrounded by mist.'

'But why love? Why love in the mist?'

'I don't know, Matti.'

———

Later, Martin helps you with the shop delivery.

'Dad's thinking of getting in some cocoa shell mulch,' he says from inside the van, sliding a plastic crate along the metal floor towards you.

'Thought he hated the smell.'

'He does. But we keep getting asked for it. Woman the other day said it keeps the cats off.'

'What? The smell?'

Martin grins and wipes his hand across his face. Today, he looks like a Polaroid photograph of himself, pale in the gloom of the van, lean and shiny and light brown like an otter.

'Fancy going out to the mill for lunch?' he asks.

———

You go single file up the narrow path to the windmill, Martin in front, surefooted and easy in his body. Drops of water bounce up off the bushes in slow motion as you disturb the branches. The air here is heavy – sweet and fumey.

The path climbs, then opens out onto the low hillside and the carcass of the old windmill. Bladeless, it's just a wooden shell, completely empty. Except, of course, there is Edward. As you approach, his pie-brown face looks down at you from the hatch at the top of the windmill. Then he looks back over his shoulder. Then he looks back at you. You can see the whites of his eyes as he heaves himself out through the hatch. Struggling with the air, he falls thirty feet, his red jacket snapping like a flag. He hits the ground front first and is suddenly still. Then he sinks into the ground.

A few seconds later, he appears back up in the hatch and does it all over again. You ignore him. It was shocking the first time you witnessed this as a child, but he has done it so many times since then; the impact wore off long ago. Now you just wish he'd move on.

Martin is walking ahead, checking the ground for rabbit poo, deciding where to sit. He doesn't know about Edward or any of the others, although you once had a short conversation about ghosts. He had been reading something, asked if you believed in them.

'Um. I don't know, really,' you hedged.

'Says here that one out of every four people says they've seen a ghost.'

You shrugged. Then your curiosity got the better of you.

'Does it say why they always appear in the same place? Why they don't wander about?'

'No.' He turned the page.

Even now, there's such a lot you don't tell Martin, although he would almost certainly describe himself as your friend. It's funny how, if you listen to people talk about themselves for long enough, they end up feeling like they know you.

———

You've always seen ghosts.

When you were a child, there was only Nanny Bee. She carried piles of fresh towels from one room to another, striding down the narrow hallway like a man, ducking her head to pass through the low doorways. She sat shelling peas at the round table in the kitchen, her bony hands as confident as anything you've ever seen. She knitted in the living room, without looking at the stitches, and whistling her breath between her teeth like a tune without noticing she was doing it.

Nanny Bee's face was like her hands, broad and bony. Her shapeless patterned dress was always clean. You took her warm, busy presence for granted, and it was a long time before you realized that your parents did not count her as part of the family, did not see her at all. But Nanny Bee was never less than real to you. She made up for the absence of any siblings. She almost made up for the fact that your parents were besotted with each other. And then, just before your thirteenth birthday, she disappeared.

For a long time, you looked for her. You called her under your breath, tried to catch her in the corner of your eye, catch her out. You even looked for her in the churchyard, although you had never seen her there before and there was no gravestone you could be sure belonged to her. Eventually you gave up. Without her, the house was emptier and colder.

It wasn't long afterwards that your mother got ill, died. That took things to a whole different level.

You started to see them everywhere then, the ghosts of people you didn't know. Random ghosts. Old, young. Ordinary people who had died. You could see them; sometimes they could see you. But the ghost of your mother never came. Eventually, you stopped looking for her, just as you had stopped looking for Nanny Bee. And now you pay little attention to those that show themselves to you from time to time. They have nothing you want. They're as insubstantial to you, now, as most living people.

———

The ground is damp, but you've forgotten the blanket again. You sit cross-legged on the long grass, and the damp seeps through your jeans, cool and soft against the backs of your thighs. You pull a stem of grass; the new growth squeaks as it slides free. You chew the tender part, the part that is sweet, and realize you're hungry. You start unwrapping your sandwich.

Martin sprawls next to you, too close, propped on one elbow. He reaches over and draws a gentle line with his thumb on the skin inside your wrist.

'Don't start, Martin,' you say. 'I'm serious. I'll get up and go back.'

He withdraws, loses interest, scans the sky with narrowed eyes. How does he do that? Connect and disconnect so easily? He reaches out and draws back as easily as the tide.

'It's clearing up,' he says. 'Sun will be back out soon. Will you be in the greenhouse again this afternoon?'

'No. It was just the nigella. And why are we doing it anyway? Why would anyone buy them as plants when they can just shake out a packet of seeds? They grow like weeds.'

'It's an order for the new garden centre on the hill. Big place.' He raises his eyebrows (seen it?) and you nod. It's a massive yellow hangar of a place, all sharp edges and angles, with an acre of tarmac for parking. People can buy table lamps there, and umbrella stands; candles and cushions; baskets for their pets to sleep in; brass doorknobs for their garden shed. That's before you even get to the plants.

'The manager told Dad the punters don't know any better,' Martin grins.

You act out a pantomime gasp, and it's not just for effect. Anyone who knows Mr Holub knows better than to speak about 'punters' or even 'customers.' You learned that the first day you arrived.

'No, no, Claire,' he'd said, rolling a cigarette between long brown fingers. 'These people here. They are not just the customer, coming to buy a *something*. They are coming to buy a growing thing. It's different, you see? They are a *gardener*.'

The Ukrainian accent gave weight to even his simplest words, but you didn't see. Not at the time. You watched people making their choices, listened to their reasons. The real gardeners touched the plants differently, with familiarity and not too gently. They knew what they were about. The rest were hopeless.

It was years before you understood – it's the plants Mr Holub respects, not the people.

That hasn't changed. He is smaller now, browner, and less interested in the running of the nursery. But he cares more than ever about the plants. When they flower, he moves them out of their allocated alphabetical slots. He arranges them in gradients of colour – blues next to mauves and lavenders. Deep purple next to magenta and red. Muttering, sometimes in English, sometimes in Ukrainian, he makes patterns of the foliage.

'This big bugger look better here.'

He contrasts spiky silver stems against a waterfall of tiny yellow leaves.

'Soft little one. Flower soon.'

He creates a backdrop of flat turquoise blades.

'Nice blue bastards.'

Mr Holub is an artist. He makes a mess of the system.

'What was Matti on about?' Martin asks. 'He said you'd been telling him about love.' He knows perfectly well, but you tell him anyway.

'Love-in-a-mist. He wanted to know about the name.'

'Names are important,' Martin says. 'They give you the essence of things.'

'Except for *people's* names,' you say.

He raises his eyebrows. You explain.

'Things get given their names to describe what they are. Right? But people are named as babies, *before* they become what they are. So they grow into their names; they turn into what they are called. Or they react against it.'

Martin tilts his head, considering the idea.

'That might be true sometimes. Having a ridiculous name could scar you for life, I can see that.'

'No. Every name. Think about it. For every name, there's a meaning. Or there's someone who owned it before you – a famous person, or a relative – to live up to.'

Martin does think about it. You have to say that for him. When you give him a chance to relate to you, he makes the effort.

'I was named after an uncle,' he says, eventually. 'My mother's brother. I have vague memories of being wheeled round to visit when I was four or five. He smelled like medicine. And his hands were white and smooth, as if they'd been wrapped in bandages all his life, or had died before the rest of him. I didn't want him to touch me.' He lifts his own brown hands in front of his face, studies them.

'He was a good man, apparently. Uncle Martin.'

He flashes a sudden grin at you.

'So what kinds of neuroses do Claires have, then?'

This is the problem. Say a bit, then people expect a bit more.

'My folks saw a movie with a Claire in it, and they liked the name.' You take a bite out of your sandwich and chew.

'That's it? What about your theory?'

'Well, it means exactly what it sounds like – 'clear.' Nothing too deep or significant.'

You had looked it up in the English-French dictionary, put an asterisk next to it.

> *A blue and red dictionary. A canvas satchel. A classroom with big windows (fenetres) and a teacher who was Canadian French not French French. A teacher who wore very smart clothes and had long, perfect fingernails. Who arrived one day with two black eyes (J'ai eu un accident). Who said, once, off-hand – 'if you're not choosing your own clothes by now, Claire, you never will' – causing a spurt of shame and hatred. Miss Cr–something. Creureur. Mademoiselle Creureur.*

'Clear is okay,' says Martin.

'Except it also means 'transparent.'

'Clear is good,' says Martin. As if you haven't spoken.

See? My name is about being invisible.

'I guess,' you say. 'Clear is fine.'

Then you say, 'Shall we go, now?'

There are flat patches in the grass where you have been sitting. But the grass is resilient. By tomorrow morning it will have sprung back up again, and no-one will be able to tell you were even here.

2

The scarf is raspberry velvet. You squeeze it, stroke it, dip your fingers into it like it's jam. You hold it against your face and breathe in the new, expensive smell of it.

When you pile it round your neck, it cups your chin. It feels kind. So you think you'll wear it for a while, just while you look around. But then when you're ready to leave, you don't want to take it off.

> I deserve this. I deserve something as soft and warm and comforting as this thing.

You let your feet carry you along the shiny floor and through the whispering automatic doors. You step into cool air and the sound of buses. You will cross the road, weave between the traffic, lose yourself in the bottleneck at the steps.

A young man's voice, anxious, close to your ear, changes everything. That reality – the one in which you get away with it – splinters off into another universe. This one leads back to the shop, back across the shiny floor, to the manager's office.

> I can just say I forgot to take it off. I can get out of this.

But the young man listens so carefully, his almost red hair is so neat and still wet where he has smoothed down the wavy bits (he is new to the job, he tells you; he hasn't actually caught anyone before; his name is Luke) that you find yourself telling more of the truth than you had planned.

He doesn't understand, although he wants to.

'Haven't you got any money?"

'Yes, I have.'

'Then if you thought you deserved it, why not just buy it for yourself?'

You can't explain. You are uncomfortable on the hard office chair, and the air in the room is too warm. It's like a little box, this room, there's barely enough space for you and Luke and the young woman who is the manager. The walls are not real walls, just thin partitions.

> Can the people in the room next door hear everything?
> Are they listening, just pretending to work?

'I just wanted a present,' you say. 'I don't know. I didn't really think any further than that.'

The manager flattens her shiny mouth into a thin line.

She's lovely. Bony in all the right places. Smooth and tanned, perfect as plastic, with no sweaty hairy bits. You find yourself staring at her legs, and shift your eyes back to her face. You run your tongue over your teeth, wishing for a split second that they were sharp, dangerous. That you could smile and make her frightened.

'I'm sorry,' you say. 'I've never done this before. Can't I just pay for the scarf and go?'

Luke looks at the manageress, raises his eyebrows.

'People can't just take things,' she says. 'We always prosecute.'

'I expect,' he says, looking miserable, 'As it's your first offence, I expect you'll just get a fine, or community service. Maybe both.'

—

Of course, it's not your first offence. When the police officers arrive, they check your bag and find the other things from the shops before this one. A wristwatch with a green suede strap. A small bottle of very expensive perfume. A pair of white cotton socks.

'Do you have receipts for these items?' asks the WPC.

You shake your head. No.

Behind her, Luke is leaning against the doorframe, looking at his feet. He is disappointed in you.

And now it begins to feel real.

There will be a process. It will be embarrassing. You feel a slow, hot blush rising up your neck.

—

Claire darling,

At last, the sun is out! The room is full of light. It's glorious! I have been so uninspired by the grey days.

You were very careful, sweetheart, when you came in with my tea this morning. Careful not to spill tea in the saucer. Careful to smile and say cheerful things. I think you've worked out exactly how you're going to get through this whole tedious process. You've always been such a funny self-contained little thing, and so sensible.

Sometimes, when your father and I were playing around, being silly like we used to, I used to feel like you were the adult, and we your children. So I think you'll be alright, sweetie. I'm sure you will.

Towards the end, she wrote the same way she breathed – struggling to get started and ending too hard – pale words that grew darker as they crossed the paper, full stops that pierced the page. But this letter comes from before that time; it's one of the early ones, still in the graceful loopy scrawl that you always admired. You try to read it with fresh eyes. There might be something new in it, something you've missed. It's the only oracle you have.

We really never knew if we'd done the right thing, having an only child. But to tell the truth, darling, I don't think I could have coped with more than one. I loved you, of course I did – but once we had you, it was enough.

I wonder might you have made friends more easily if you'd grown up with brothers and sisters? You spend so much time on your own.

Then again, I had four siblings, and there was never enough of anything to go round. None of us got enough attention and there was never enough money. I'm glad you didn't have to share everything like I did. I was very happy, having your father and you, just the three of us.

This isn't helping. You wish you had chosen a different one, but there are rules about that. To choose, you have to kneel and shut your eyes and empty your mind. You have to run the tips of your fingers across the ridges of the envelopes. When you feel the right one, the one that makes your fingers tingle, you can take it out. You have to read it all the way through.

I hope you find that kind of happiness one day, sweetie. My wish is that you'll find someone to love as deeply as I love your father – and when you find that person, don't let anything or anybody stand in the way. It is the best thing in the world, my darling, being married to a man you adore.

No. This really isn't helping.

I'll stop now, sweetheart. I'm getting tired.

It's signed, like all the others, *Your Loving Mother* even though you always called her 'Mum.' This still jars a bit, leaves you faintly surprised.

The first few times you read it, the letter made you angry. You had a response, in your head, for every line.

> I *had* to be self-contained. You and Dad were so totally wrapped up in each other.

> There wasn't enough to go round, even with only the three of us.

> It was *you* that didn't want to share.

But those things don't seem as important now. You're not even sure anymore whether they're true. Now you are reading for clues.

Did she know, when she wrote this?

Did she plan this far in advance?

But between the lines there are just spaces where nothing is said.

You put the paper to your nose as if there might be answers hidden in the smell of it. If they were ever there, they have leaked away; you might even have breathed them in already without knowing.

And as for anything to help you deal with the old woman tomorrow – nothing. You have simply been reminded: Be glad you are on your own. Be grateful you don't have to deal with your father's disappointment and your mother's support.

You fold the thick paper, re-file the envelope randomly, catch the scent of wood polish as you close the box.

—

3

It's a wide avenue, tree-lined, leading from the station down to the sea. And long. The horizon shines at the end like a distant country. During the night, the wind has brought down a layer of new leaves, left them gasping on the pavement, soft under your shoes. You are walking down a wide avenue, on a carpet of leaves, under elms planted two hundred years ago. On your left, the road is bright and hard, but here on the pavement, the shade is kind, the air smells of ivy and damp brick.

Oh god. This is going to be awful.

You watch your steps, consider the colours passing in slow motion under your feet. Moss green. Stone grey. Clay brown. A bird unravels small spirals of sound in the branches above you.

You imagine being able wrap a shell around each of the painful thoughts and feelings within you, a soft papery shell that would harden with time. You imagine a clutch of pale eggs resting inside your head. You wonder if there would be room for them all.

The Magistrate's Court had been painful. You had never been in a courtroom before. This one was disappointing, something like a theatre, but modern and shabby. Instead of a stage at the front, there was a high wooden desk built right across the room. Seated behind it, the three magistrates looked small. You had to tilt your head to look up at them.

You sat on a grubby plastic seat in one of the back rows, finding it hard to breathe, waiting your turn. A tall man in a light suit was explaining – he hadn't really been speeding, just unfamiliar with the area. You didn't believe him. His voice sounded thin.

The magistrates were all women, and ordinary. One was younger, bright haired; one round-faced with a bob; one angular with short grey hair, an orange scarf at her neck.

You had expected men, stern and punitive. You had armoured yourself against harsh words and expected not to care what they thought of you. But faced with these pleasant women, you found yourself feeling ashamed.

When it was your turn, they listened carefully as the Crown Prosecutor read the police report. Several items of significant value. Fifty four previous offences to be taken into account, dating back to the early death of your mother. He read without any feeling at all, but slowly and clearly. The woman with bright hair asked if you had anything to add.

'Just that I really won't do it again,' you said. Your voice sounded thin, too.

The women whispered amongst themselves, too quietly to be heard. The air conditioning rattled. A tiny green light blinked on a camera mounted on the wall in the corner.

The woman with the scarf spoke then. The fact you had done it regularly – not often, but regularly over the months, building up the pile of bags and bundles under your bed – that made it more serious. One solitary act would have been different. Then again, you had returned every item, every single thing. They could take that into account. They were required to respond with a suitable sentence, not just a punishment, something that would serve the community.

Moss. Green. Clay. Brown. You have slowed almost to a standstill. Looking at the houses this end of the avenue, it's hard to imagine this community needs serving. These houses are bigger than they have any right to be. Four and five storeys of yellow brick, they crouch over the pavement, sulking over their multiple doorbells. But none of them is the house you are looking for. *The big red house – roses at front.* The woman from Probation had printed it carefully under the address on a piece of paper.

'Your timing is great – I've just had these details in,' she had been excited on your behalf, keen to sort you out, nibbling at her full bottom lip with small front teeth as she scanned the page.

'There's a new project for suitable offenders. Look, here it is,' the lip puckered, pleased. 'You'd be spending time with elderly people who need help in their homes,' she glanced up over her glasses, checking for a response – *could you do that?* You shrug, nod. 'Or visiting vulnerable people who are isolated for one reason or another' – *ok with that?* You nod again.

'Great! You have to be assessed, we can't send just anybody, but I can go through that with you now and I think you'll be perfect…'

At the tall iron gate, you check the address again. The paper is damp now, soft and warm in the palm of your hand. You open your fingers and let it fall. Of course; it had to be this house. The biggest house; the only one like it.

It's a crazy house. Terracotta in every shade from ancient red to pale apricot, it shines out from beneath layers of old soot, bright between the grime etched into its nooks and crannies. Every surface is embellished; there's no restraint here. Neither is there any symmetry:

On the right, three enormous bay windows, one on top of another, glazed with lozenge shaped panes that catch the light, distort its reflections.

On the left, something like a turret, four storeys high, with tiles that overlap like scales and long narrow windows of curved glass. You wonder about the mysterious manufacturing process involved in that, the logistics of shaping and fitting glass that curves. You wonder what it is like to look out from inside.

Above, the roof erupts into pointed dormers, awkward angles, tiny windows tucked into obscure corners. And it all hangs together somehow, finds its own equilibrium, between three huge chimneys on one side, and two smaller ones on the other.

A seagull gabbles from the rooftop as you step through the cold iron gate and along the narrow path between the old shrubbery of the front garden, up three steps onto the island that is the porch.

And here are the roses. Nothing like the soft pink sprawl of Blush Noisette around your own door (floppy, only mildly spiteful), these stems are old. They coil through the ironwork, thick serpents with spines as straight and sharp as needles. Dozens of tight narrow buds squat amongst the dark green foliage.

Nasty.

There is only one doorbell. Round and black, set in a circle of patterned terracotta plaster, it resists the pressure of your finger. Then it bleats faintly somewhere inside the house.

Almost immediately, the door opens a few inches.

You speak into the gap: 'I'm Claire Farrell. I've come to see Mrs Bell.'

The door swings inwards, releases a strong smell of furniture polish, reveals a heavy woman, quite a lot older than you, maybe in her fifties. Her pale brown hair is scraped back so tight it hurts just to look at it; the harsh style gives her fleshy face and thick features nowhere to hide. You almost miss her eyes, but she darts a glance at you, and it's a surprise. They are beautiful: large and dark and long-lashed below finely-drawn eyebrows. Then she looks down, becomes lumpy and nondescript again.

You scrabble in your bag, grab your shiny copy of *Jane Eyre*.

'I've come to read to her. Mrs Bell?'

She scowls and steps back, making space for you in the beeswax-laden hallway. It's a big hallway, but dark, all the doors along its length closed firmly shut. You follow as she leads you towards the back of the house, then up a heavy stairway, the grey flannel of her jog pants stretching tight across her wide haunches with every step.

That's one hell of a backside.

Is it an act of confidence? To lead the way up the stairs. To make your behind so visible.

Is it an act of trust?

Maybe she just doesn't care.

On the half-landing, an arched window offers a glimpse of the back garden, dominated by old trees, wildly overgrown. More stairs, then she pushes through the first door on the left.

'How many times do you have to be told, Margaret? Knock. Do you understand me? Knock on the door before you come in!'

It's a strong voice. The voice of an actress or a teacher. A voice that reminds you of stones – grey granite or silvery quartz – polished until they shine. You follow Margaret through the doorway, expecting someone imposing. But it's a small person propped up on velvet pillows in the bed opposite the window. A small still woman.

When she speaks to you, her words are warmer and perfectly shaped. Jasper, tiger's eye. Semi-precious stones strung together. 'Hello, my dear. Welcome. I don't suppose you have been properly introduced to Margaret Keyes, my housekeeper? She takes care of me, after a fashion. But she has no manners.'

Before you can respond, Margaret Keyes has turned and left the room, smacking the door shut behind her.

'Don't pay her the least bit of attention.' The small person smiles, and is suddenly charming. 'So you are Claire Farrell.

And I am Eveline Bell. Eve-linn. Not Ev-aline. And I prefer Evie.'

Mrs Bell, Evie, is not what you'd imagined. Not a frail and elderly invalid. Not vague and refined. She is pale, true enough, and slight. And she must be seventy. But she is *vital*. Pixie-faced, with a short crop of silver hair and unusually light brown eyes, there is a kind of tension about her. She is alert, intent, and not in the least bit child-like; the pixieness is more ancient than that, more of a force to be reckoned with.

There's something well-drawn about her features. Nothing tentative or smudged; the bone isn't far beneath the skin. And she is one of those women with high arched eyebrows, with enough space to create shimmering butterfly wings of colour above her eyes, although she is wearing no makeup at all. It gives her an air of openness, as if she has nothing to hide.

'And you can put that away.'

Her body is perfectly motionless, but she has tilted her head slightly and is looking at the book in your hand.

Oh my god I forgot.

She can't move.

You wave the book, floundering.

'It's *Jane Eyre* – I thought it might...'

'Oh no, I don't intend to be read to. If I'm to have you here, dear, I want your company. We won't need to fill the space with anyone else's words. I have plenty of my own – and I'm sure you do, too.' She laughs, loudly, the sound of crystals forming. You put the book back in your bag as you approach the bed.

It is like a sleigh. The dark wood curves high at the head, lower at the foot, solid and smooth. There is a device on the headboard, something technical. Perhaps an intercom, so she can call the housekeeper when she needs something. The bedspread is velvet, patterned purple and blue.

'Sit yourself down; there, on the end,' says Evie. 'It's easier for me if I don't have to turn my head.'

Under the layer of velvet, the mattress crackles and puffs slightly as you sit. Like something inflated; like plastic. You lean back against the footboard, your knees pulled up and to the side, so your shoes don't touch the covers.

'Well, what do you think?'

You look around the room, taking in the clutter of furniture and ornament. The walls, where you can see them, are turquoise, but there are dozens of pictures, some framed, others tatty-edged canvases, even pages ripped from magazines. There's a painting above the bed, a soft, curved naked woman in an elaborate frame.

There are no bare surfaces. The enormous marble mantelpiece is crowned with peacock feathers, hung with tiny brass bells, host to a small herd of unidentifiable objects. The book cases sag under double rows of books. The massive wardrobe is so full the doors splay open, spilling jewel-coloured fabrics. A freestanding clothes rail bends under the weight of more silk, velvet, and chiffon. There is a green sofa, an ornate coffee table. And on the floor, oriental rugs overlap in peacock shades, creating a patchwork of fine silk stitches, a hundred years' worth of work and ruined eyesight.

Everything beyond the bed is slightly dusty, and there's a sweet, musty smell. Not unpleasant; a trace of perfume, old and expensive.

'It's nice. Interesting.'

Evie laughs. She's genuinely amused.

'No, not the room. What do you think of me? The invalid woman. Am I what you were expecting? Am I a surprise?'

You are fascinated by the fluidity of her face. Every word is beautifully shaped by her lips, accompanied by a raised eyebrow, a narrowing of the eyes, as though her face makes up for the immobility of her body. You don't want to look at her body. The slight, still shape beneath the covers; the pale, motionless arms.

'Paralysed,' the woman from Probation had explained 'Or as good as.' She had tucked in her bottom lip sympathetically. 'She hasn't been able to get out of bed at all for the last six months, poor dear.'

But even bedridden, Evie is stylish. She is wearing a silk shirt – a kind of tunic, deep green, embroidered at the neck. And she is wearing several silver rings, one with a large turquoise stone.

'I didn't really know what to expect,' you say. 'But I guess I imagined you would look more... ill.'

'They haven't told you what's wrong with me?'

'No. Just that you're... That you can't move.'

'Ah. Then, my dear, you know as much as I do.' She smiles. 'Shall I tell you what the doctors say? What some of the best medical minds in the country have come up with?'

Not a rhetorical question. She waits for you to nod.

'They say there is nothing wrong with me! Isn't this astonishing? One can progressively lose all movement and feeling, starting with numbness in the feet and hands, stumbling, dropping things. One can end up almost entirely still, trapped in a bed with a sour old spinster as nurse and caretaker. And for no physical reason! It's psychosomatic, they say. They say I don't *want* to move.'

You don't know how to respond. This is very close. You have not invited this woman to take you into her confidence. And then again, you're curious – in the same way you were drawn as a child, to what lived underneath things. You had turned over rocks and tree stumps, purposefully disturbing the small creatures that were not meant to be seen by you or anyone else. They had wriggled or scuttled or slid away, certain of their need to be hidden.

'Do you think that's true? That you don't want to move?'

Evie takes a breath, in through her nose, out through her mouth. Her head tilted to one side, she thinks about it.

'It might be,' she says.

Then she says nothing at all for a while, simply waits.

You doodle on the velvet cover with the tip of your finger, causing a tiny disturbance in the grain of the fabric, a little whirlpool going the wrong way.

In the silence, the clock on the wall seems unnecessarily loud, demanding attention. You don't want to look at it directly – that would be like saying 'How much longer do I have to be here?' That would be rude. But you can see it at the edge of your vision, a wooden box of a clock, twitching its tail in slow motion.

So loud. Like a heartbeat. But heavier.

You feel your own heartbeat slow down to match its rhythm. You feel hot, slightly sick.

'My dear, you aren't comfortable.' You look up to find her eyes still on you.

'No, I'm fine, really. Just a bit hot.' You flap your hand, fan yourself.

And still she doesn't look away. Most people back off when they see a 'Keep Out' sign, even a subtle one. They pretend they haven't seen it, but they back off anyway, as if it were their own idea to turn around. This woman doesn't seem to have the same boundaries as other people. You feel her eyes on you even as you look away towards the window. You feel the pause. And eventually, you hear the breath she takes before speaking.

'Do you know what I think, Claire? I think perhaps you were planning to come here and spend a couple of hours killing time. Turn up once a week for as long as you have to, read out loud to the old lady, go home... I think you intended to simply get through it, without ever finding out who I am, or showing me who you are.'

Your spine straightens; the muscles between your ribs stiffen into armour. But Evie arches her eyebrows, making pale furrows of her forehead, and you have to say *something*. So you clip your words, make them tight and formal.

'I apologise. I'm not entirely comfortable around illness.'

'Ah. So if I were well, you'd be comfortable?'

She waits, but you say nothing; she continues.

'I don't think so, my dear. I have quite a strong feeling that perhaps you *live* at arms' length. Which is a shame, because I've been lying here on my own for long enough to know what that feels like. But, truthfully, I'd rather be on my own than go through the motions with someone who doesn't want to be here.'

A flare of anger rises in your chest, heats the words that come out of your mouth.

'You've only just met me. You can't possibly know that much about me.'

She smiles. 'Oh, you'd be surprised how much people reveal about themselves. It's all in the details, Claire. I've spent a lifetime noticing the details. You've held your hands in fists since you arrived.'

You look down at your hands. Unclench them.

'Perhaps you need to go home and think about it, my dear. If you're determined to kill time, I'm sure the agency can find you a more conventional invalid to visit.'

She turns her head, nudges one of the padded buttons on the intercom with her jaw.

'After all, this first meeting was an opportunity for both of us to find out whether we'd suit each other. There's no shame in deciding it won't work. I do hope, though, that you decide to risk coming out from behind that wall of yours. I have a feeling that the person behind it is well worth knowing.'

You are looking each other in the eye, now. She doesn't blink and you don't look away.

> Alright. If you really want to know what's behind the wall. Take a good look.

> I don't like the way you are intruding.

> I don't like *you*.

Then there are trudging footsteps on the stairs, and someone bangs on the door, hard enough to make it shake. Evie breaks into laughter.

'Margaret Keyes is making a point, the stupid woman.' She winks at you, then raises her voice – 'Yes, come in!'

'Claire is ready to leave now,' she tells Margaret Keyes, who is looking surly. And to you – 'I do, very much, hope to see you next Wednesday. Thank you for coming, Claire.'

You follow Margaret down the staircase, past the arched window, along the wide dark hallway to the front door. She opens the door without saying a word, but glances at you sideways, slyly triumphant. Definitely triumphant. That look isn't collusive. It doesn't mean *See what I have to put up with?* It doesn't mean *Don't worry, I know what she's like.* Margaret Keyes is glad to be rid of you.

Through the door and onto the porch, the air is cool against your hot face. You take a few deep breaths. Your hands, on the latch of the iron gate, are shaking.

You don't need to think about it.

You already know you won't be coming back.

—

– 4 –

You had been washing up, looking out the kitchen window, watching sparrows argue in the pear tree while you tried to talk yourself out of looking at another letter.

But the last one didn't help at all.

No. It's too soon.

But here you are anyway, on your knees in front of the writing bureau, your hands still wet and soapy. You wipe them on your jeans before opening the box.

Dearest Claire,

Not feeling strong today. Watching the sky through my window. I know there are people out there, going on with their lives. But my whole life is in this room now. I see only your father's dear face, and yours. The nurses don't count.

I've been thinking about the way we used to shut out the rest of the world, your father and I. I wonder if we knew, somehow. That we wouldn't have long. But you have all the time in world, my darling. Don't be alone.

I want you to be happy, Claire. I love you.

You refold the page, hold it against your forehead for a moment before putting it away. The creamy paper is smooth and cool, like your mother's hands before she got ill. Around you, the room is hazy with evening sunlight. More considerate, you think, than daytime sunlight. It hesitates; it doesn't just barge in.

You put the letter away and slide across the floor to lean against the old brown leather sofa. Tipping your head back, you scan the walls and ceiling. Even in this gentle light, it's obvious the room needs redecorating. The walls are several different shades of grey; the empty bookshelves are grimy.

This room used to be lined with books. Your father took his favourites when he left; you got rid of the rest as soon as you could. The charity shop collected them. Boxes and boxes of books, good books. The volunteers couldn't understand why you didn't want to sell them. But you just wanted them gone. They had been your parents' shared passion; exclusive. They read out loud to each other, or they read the same book at once; your mother curled against him, reading over his shoulder. 'Ready?' he would ask, and wait for her to catch up before turning the page.

Now the shelves are pointless. You should take them down; it would make the room seem bigger. You run your hand over the thin carpet, over the blues and greys, the faded flashes of pink that have always reminded you of salmon gleaming in shallow water.

The 'study', they called it. There is a desk here, plain and solid. The soft leather sofa. And a small mahogany writing bureau that once belonged to your father's brother. The lid folds down, reveals vertical compartments for letters and paperwork. As a child, you thought of this as 'the magic cupboard.' It was full of writing paper, pencils and pens, postcards, envelopes. Now it holds only two things: the wooden box containing your mother's letters, and the dictionary your father gave you.

I want you to be happy, Claire. I love you.

It's confusing. You had been so certain that she wanted you out of the house, out in the world, so she could be alone with your father. Now you don't know. Perhaps she really had been thinking about what was good for you. You conjure an image of yourself, small Claire, happily roaming the country-side, one of the loud band of village children. You imagine coming home tired and dirty, and being welcome, because they had had enough time without you – time enough, even, to miss you. But it hadn't been like that.

I hovered, always too close.

No. Worse than that.

I intruded.

You get up on your knees, pull open the lid of the writing bureau, grab the dictionary and flick through the pages. Most have a small black line drawing to illustrate one of the words. *Bark* is illustrated. *Grapefruit. Sundial. Turtle.* As a child, you had almost been sure that they changed, those pictures. That while the book was closed, the old words gave up their little etchings and new words had their turn. Your father brought the dictionary home with him one day. You must have been about nine.

'I've got something for you.'

He revealed it from behind his back, unwrapped, more special than a birthday present. He showed you how it worked, how you could find exactly the word you wanted simply by tracking it down, one letter at a time. How it told you exactly what the words meant.

'Is every word in here?' you asked.

'Perhaps not every word. But probably all the words you'll need for quite a while.'

He showed you how the symbols helped you pronounce unfamiliar words. The ones you'd never heard before. *Abacus. Barrage. Citadel.*

'It's good to know lots of words, isn't it, Dad?'

'It certainly is. The more words you know, the more chance you have of saying exactly what you mean.' And you had believed him, although you know differently now.

You sink into the leather sofa, lie flat with your head supported on one padded arm, your feet on the other, the dictionary perched open on your chest.

Intrusion. An 'act of forcing in.' An 'unwelcome visit.' Personally, you would have defined intrusion as a more subtle thing – a stubborn invasion of sly increments.

There's a legal definition too: 'unlawful entry.'

And a geological definition: about 'molten rock forced into underground spaces.'

See:

> *A porridge of lava heaving itself into the tiny gap between two wafers of silver rock. There is no room for it, but it keeps coming. The silver rock wrinkles and gives way.*

See:

> *Baby sparrows squeezed to the outside edges of the nest as a cuckoo baby grows fat amongst them, monstrous and uncaring.*

Then the perspective flips. *You* are the cuckoo baby. And you do care. You don't want to be monstrous.

The sparrow babies wheeze resentment; it hangs like a cloud around you.

You have all the time in world, my darling. Don't be alone.

You close the dictionary sharply, stand up and replace it in the bureau. The light is fading now, the room colder. You will redecorate in here – dismantle the shelves, fill the holes, paint the walls. You'll do it soon.

———

5

'**D**o you want to come with me to look at a mushroom farm?'

You finish dipping the last of the three-inch pots and place them on the draining board, then turn around. Martin is leaning against the doorframe, comfortable, as though he's been there for some time. You wonder how long he's been watching you. It's a tedious job, scraping out the residue and cobwebs with a stiff brush, dipping each pot into a sterilising solution so it can be re-used. But you don't mind it. The sink is right by the greenhouse door, there's a breeze. You like the thin ribs of shadow that criss-cross the concrete floor.

'What for?' you ask.

'Just to have a look round.'

'Yes, but why? Are you thinking about growing mushrooms?'

He hooks his thumbs into his jeans pockets, shrugs. His forearms are already brown.

'Why not? I'm looking into it. We've got plenty of room here. We should be developing.'

'But you don't actually need me to come, do you?'

'Oh don't be such a misery, Claire. I've arranged it with the farm manager. He's going to show us around next Friday.'

'I haven't said I want to go yet, Martin. I'll think about it.' You turn away, turn the tap back on.

The bath is not long enough; you can't straighten your legs; your knees stick out like bony islands, pale and uninhabited. The inflatable plastic cushion cradles your head; the mirror at the end of the bath reflects you back to yourself. You have seen articles in magazines about the shape of faces. The most desirable shape, apparently, is a perfect oval. Your face is oval, but narrower and longer than in the magazines. You scowl into the mirror. Your hair and eyes are too dark, or too matte, they seem to absorb the light rather than reflect it. The strands that reach your shoulders have a half-curl. You wonder if you can get away without washing it again. Probably not. Uninspired, you close your eyes and sink a little so your ears are under the water.

The world changes then, the sound of your own body closes in on you. Breathing becomes the sea, waves of air crash into the shores of your lungs and recede. Inside you, something gurgles; a spring of sound. And behind that, your heart beats, echoing through the chambers of your chest into the surrounding water.

The girls at school said if you could put a pencil under your breasts – and it stayed there – you needed to wear a bra. Breasts that pinned the pencil down, held it snug against your ribcage, were too big or too saggy to go without. Even now, you can't hold a pencil under your breasts. Pearl Andersen could, even when she was only thirteen. She had beautiful lacy bras, white and crisp, and a red one she wore at weekends. You didn't mind. They looked pretty but uncomfortable.

The water creeps over your chin, hovers beneath your mouth. You play with the feel of it, bobbing your head so that the edge of the water rises and falls against your lips like something solid.

Pearl shared her lunch with you once. Sitting on the short dry grass outside the classrooms, she broke her sandwich in half, her biscuit, her apple. Meticulously fair, she offered each piece like a gift. And you did the same, dividing your sandwich, your carrot and celery sticks, your tangerine, breathlessly, like you were taking part in a ritual. The sun bounced off the windows of the classrooms; you felt it pierce your chest, warm as a flare, and seep down through your organs. You were filled with light, invincible, while the other girls, excluded, ate their own lunches. Pearl took small bites, her teeth white and pointy, and licked her lips with the tip of her tongue. And then, next lunchtime, she shared her lunch with someone else.

You realised then that the light had been hers, yours to borrow for a short while only. You learned to be careful about accepting borrowed light, because of the cold place left when it was withdrawn.

Pearl knew she had that light. She had bestowed it and withdrawn it consciously, testing the boundaries of her power. Martin has never done it that way. He doesn't deliberately play at casting people back into the shadows.

And still.

Martin had been seventeen when you met him on your first day at the nursery. He had seemed so much more grown up than you, so sure of himself. Maybe because he was Mr Holub's son, so he belonged there. But also because that's just how he was. You were sixteen, learning to live with your mother's illness; and then with her death. You weeded the front bed together; Martin showed you how to tell the difference between the weeds and the plants and told you their names – the soft furry lamb's ears of the stachys, and the pointy silver-leafed echinops.

'My Dad loves these,' he had said, rubbing the ball of his thumb over a velvety white stachys leaf. 'They flower purple. The echinops will be purple too – amazing, spiky like a rolled-up hedgehog.'

Martin was assured. He was steady. And that had been so necessary then, when your father felt so insubstantial, as if he had half-followed your mother.

You didn't like the person you had to be when you were at home. But Martin was normal and he made you feel normal. You loved his openness, his freeflow conversation. You loved the way he was fine even when you were silent – when you couldn't think what to say; or when you couldn't say what you were thinking.

You were acutely aware of him. When he wasn't watching, you stared. You noted the way his t-shirt pulled across his back when he lifted things. The way his skin shone when he sweated. When you were working in different parts of the nursery, whatever you were doing, you felt his presence like a current of air. It lifted the hairs on your arms.

'Can I tell you something?' he asked one day while you were tagging up new shrubs together. You heard a new level of intimacy in his voice, a deeper, softer note that made you look up, expecting something.

'I kissed Rachel Payne last weekend,' he said. And grinned. You blinked. A slow-motion shuttering that gave you just enough time to make your eyes flat and careless. There were other people in Martin's life. Of course there were. You pulled back the part of you that had been growing towards him, shrunk your feelings.

Now, years later, Martin feels something more for you. But you don't know how to go back to the place where you were open to that.

You think about the trip to the mushroom farm, whether to go. And about Evie's smile, the light in Evie's eyes.

It's not about trusting people.

Sooner or later, they all take their light back.

It's about whether I can trust myself to bear it when they do.

You slip down further into the bath to wet your hair. The water is exactly the same temperature as your blood.

———

'Won't be a minute,' says Martin, heading for the office to find the manager. You wait outside in the car park, leaning against the van, enjoying the feel of the warm metal against your back and tilting your face to sniff the air. It doesn't smell mushroomy, even this close to the huge polythene growing tunnels. There must be a dozen tunnels lined up under the sky like a row of beached whales. They're bigger than real tunnels, easily wide enough to swallow four lanes of traffic – but instead of burrowing through hillsides, they loom above ground, their grey polythene skin stretched tight over metal ribs.

Then Martin is back, introduces you to Andy, who is tall, blond and serious, with narrow eyes and a narrow face. He is wearing a bright yellow lab coat and a navy blue hat. You have to wear them too, he says. You struggle into one of the thick cotton coats and fiddle uncertainly with the hairnet that's attached to the hat.

'Just tuck it under,' he says, over his shoulder. The two of them are already off down the road between the polytunnels, Andy efficient, Martin eager. You lag behind, enjoying the strangeness of it, of being funnelled between two huge curved polythene walls. When you catch up with them at the compost yard, Martin is asking about the mix of horseshit to straw. But even surrounded by steaming hills of compost, you still can't smell anything.

'This is the heating chamber,' says Andy, standing in front of a concrete shed. 'We sterilise trays of compost in here then saturate them with mushroom spawn.' When he opens the chamber, the aroma of cooking compost rushes out. You edge closer to get a glimpse, but the chamber is dark and Andy shuts the door before your eyes adjust.

He leads the way to the nearest polytunnel and slides back a heavy metal door, releasing a new smell, a raw, sweet stink that blooms like a primeval flower in the back of your throat. It's pitch black. Then he turns on the light and you're looking over row upon row of compost-filled trays stacked three deep.

Andy picks up a handful of wet compost the colour of coffee grounds. He pokes at it with a latex covered finger, points out the strands of feathery white mould running through it.

'Takes fourteen days for the spawn to colonise the compost,' he says.

In the next tunnel, the trays are more advanced, the smell sweeter and lighter.

'Look.' You are startled by Andy's voice, suddenly close.

'Here.' He's pointing at something in the tray. 'You can see where the mushrooms will form. These little blobs. Called 'pins'.'

You can't see anything, but it seems important to him.

'Here,' he says, pointing at another one. You nod and smile.

Andy calls to Martin and shepherds you both out the far end of the tunnel into a busy corridor; men and women in yellow coats move along it in both directions. It reminds you of a science fiction movie, although you can't remember which one.

I Married a Killer Mushroom.

You smirk, enjoying your own joke – the fact that you've made one – even though it's hardly funny.

'This is the central corridor. The tunnels all open off from here.' Andy leads the way through one of the doors. When he turns on the light, you see that these are not mushrooms. Not yet. But the trays have become a breeding ground where hundreds of tiny shapes are swelling, thicker at the base than the top.

'At this stage, they double their size every twenty four hours,' says Andy.

Hard to believe these inert little lumps are growing that quickly. There is no sign of striving.

'Does it set them back, having the light on?' you ask, and Andy smiles for the first time.

'They don't actually need to be in the dark. They grow just as well in the sun. We turn off the lights to save electricity.'

You are surprised. 'They really don't care one way or the other?'

'Nope. They don't have any chlorophyll' – he raises his eyebrows to check you know what chlorophyll is, and you nod – 'that's why we can grow them in layers like this. The ones underneath don't try to reach for the light like green plants would.'

He turns off the switch as we exit the tunnel.

'It's just us that need the light,' he says. 'Come on, I'll show you the next batch; they were ready this morning.'

At last: proper mushrooms, white and textured like eggshell, slightly flaky around the brim. This tunnel is brightly lit.

Wearing hairnets, the pickers move amongst the trays, bobbing and dipping. You watch as the woman nearest to you grasps a mushroom with the tips of blue latex fingers, so gently, so tenderly, she might be blind. She twists carefully. Pulls. The mushroom pops out of its compost bed, a clump of dark earth clinging to a stump like the end of a broken bone. She uses a small knife to snick off the rough end, puts the freshly picked mushroom into a plastic crate on the floor. It takes only seconds; she bends towards the next one.

'Does it make your back ache?' you ask.

'No,' she answers, her hands still busy. 'Although with me so tall, you'd think it would.'

Then she shows you her knife, which has a curved blade, an orange plastic handle. 'We all have our own knives,' she says, pointing to a number stamped into the blade. She picks another mushroom, in slow-motion so you can see the technique.

'Thank you,' you say. She nods and ducks down to reach the bottom layer.

'Are you done, Claire?' Martin calls. 'We're going to see the packing.'

On the way out, you pass a bin full of larger mushrooms, with open gills and twisted stems. 'Some we didn't pick in time,' explains Andy. 'You only have to be a day late.'

In the van, on the way home, Martin talks a lot about the technical aspects of growing mushrooms. He tells you they still have to be picked by hand because no-one has invented a machine that can do it without damaging them.

'Apparently, they're working on a design that sucks the mushrooms out of the ground,' he says, enthusiastic.

You think about the tender searching fingers, the graceful turning of the wrist, that you have seen today.

'Did you enjoy it?' asks Martin. 'Are you glad you came?'

'Yes I am, thanks. I found it interesting.'

'Which bit?' He glances sideways, his pale blue eyes curious.

'Lots of it,' you say. 'The whole process. Especially the fact that they don't have to be grown in the dark.'

Although that's not quite it. It's their indifference to the light you find fascinating. That they don't reach for it, even when it's there.

'You came back then.' Margaret Keyes speaks in flat, heavy tones and you realize you never heard her voice last time. It's the colour of dishwater, but not liquid. More like a blanket, thick and heavy; it suits her body but contradicts her extraordinary eyes. Now she blocks the doorway, soft and large in grey jogpants and sweatshirt, and you wonder if she intends to keep you out. You're standing close enough to see the pores in her skin, the faint shadow of blue veins in her throat.

'Yes, I've come back.' Your own voice comes out flat and heavy, matches hers, and you realize it *is* a blanket, a thick layer intended to stifle something that would otherwise flutter and warble. You clear your throat.

'May I come in?'

She steps back silently into the dim hallway. Following her this time you notice your own hard footsteps; the entrance is tiled in terracotta. Deeper into the hallway, your footsteps disappear into the runner of carpet that climbs the stairs.

'For God's sake, Margaret, go away. She knows the way now – you don't have to hold her hand.'

Evie's scowl makes her look older and more ordinary. She watches Margaret leave, and when the door is closed, turns her eyes to you. And now she is smiling. And now she doesn't look ordinary at all.

You had forgotten how small she is. Somehow, she has taken on huge proportions in your mind over the past week. It's a shock to see how little a disturbance her body makes in the velvet covered bed. Without being told, you sit on the end, so she won't have to turn her head to see you.

'Hello.' Your fingers seek out the familiar crushed softness of the velvet. You breathe in the sweet spicy smell that haunts the room. Evie is wearing purple today, the red glowing purple of ripe Victoria plums. The mandarin collar is loose around her neck; her skin is so pale and thin it makes the silk look heavy.

'So what do you think?' she asks.

You take a deep breath and tell her what you think.

'You're younger than I expected. You don't look ill. And you don't smell like a sick person.'
Your chest is hammering. Evie says nothing, and you go on.

'You don't behave like a sick person, either. You're pushy. Intrusive. You're rude to Margaret Keyes. And I don't like the way you insist, as if you have a right to know my thoughts. You don't have a right. It's up to me whether I talk about them.'

Another deep breath.

'But you were right when you said I live at arm's length. I make sure no-one gets too close. Even though a part of me really wants someone to get close enough to see me and know who I am. So, I wasn't going to come back. And then I realized that if I don't do something different, nothing will change.'

Your voice is shaking but you swallow and carry on speaking.

'I do want something to change. I do want something more.'
You frown.

'And if I really don't like it – if it feels too hard – I can always walk away, can't I? You can't follow me.'

Your palms are damp. On some level you notice how much physical effort it requires to simply tell the truth.

And Evie is still smiling.

'Hello, Claire,' she says. 'I am truly delighted to see you.'

—

6

Sweetheart,

You've been so busy today with your plants. You came in at lunchtime and showed me the little geraniums you brought home from the nursery. Pelargoniums, you called them. You told me that geraniums are the wrong name even though everyone uses it. You were so correct about it, darling.

You've been outside digging and planting all afternoon. I'm glad you enjoy it so much, although I'd love to see you do something a bit more sociable (but I won't nag). I never was much of a gardener myself, I liked the wilderness around the house. The wild flowers and ferns. It was one of the things that won us over, your father and I, when we were looking at houses before you were born. It made the house seem more secret, more magical, as though time might stand still here, with us happily tucked away inside.

Of course, time has moved on. You arrived. Now I am leaving. Although I plan to hold on for as long as I can, of course, to have as many more moments with you and your father as possible. It might be easier to let go if I believed I was going to the 'better place' people talk about. But you know, don't you darling, that I've never believed in that sort of thing. No spirit; no soul to go on after death. I'll simply be absorbed into the earth and the air and become tiny pieces of the whole world again.

I remember telling you that a few years ago. But you were convinced I was wrong. 'It doesn't happen like that,' you told me. You were absolutely certain. But when I asked how you could be so sure, you wouldn't say. 'I just know,' you said.

Well, my darling, whatever happens, I want you to know that I have been very happy. And I am trying very hard to feel grateful for what I have been allowed, although it's difficult not to feel cheated. I am going to be as brave as I can, and I know you will be, too.

All my love.

———

Margaret Keyes has started making tea for you. She didn't ask how you liked it, just produced it on your third visit, interrupting your session with Evie to thump across the soft carpets while you watched in surprised silence. With one hand, she pulled an ornate square side table close to you at the end of the bed and banged the teacup down in the middle of it.

'Tea,' she stated, and left you to it.

Very weak, with a lot of milk, it lay thick and pale in the china cup – what your mother used to call 'teddy bear tea.' If you drink it while it's hot, it's not too bad.

Evie drinks lemonade, made fresh every day. 'It doesn't keep well,' she says, and insists that Margaret squeezes new lemons each morning. You saw her send it back last time, after just one taste.

'Take this away, Margaret. It's yesterday's. Did you think I wouldn't know?'

Margaret didn't even protest. Just picked up the glass and took it away, but you thought, as she turned, you saw the pucker of a smile at the edge of her mouth.

'Stupid woman,' said Evie. 'If she had any sense at all, she'd know. I always notice.' You hear the knot of annoyance in Evie's voice, picture it lodged in her windpipe.

I think she does know. Doesn't care.

Maybe even does it on purpose.

Today, though, the lemonade is acceptable. The plastic glass perches on a shelf close to Evie's head, so she can turn her face and sip from the straw. The liquid gleams. You wonder if it's sour, or whether Margaret adds sugar to sweeten it.

This is your fifth visit. Not including the first time, which doesn't count. You only started counting from the day you came back, on Evie's terms, willing to be seen.

That day, you stood at the gate gathering courage, feeling more like you were about to face a tidal wave than a tiny old woman who could not move. You anticipated the wave breaking over you, abrasive, scrubbing away your skin and tissues; sucking them away to feed bluntfaced fishes.

But it didn't.

So you know now that the wave does not flay you; it just scrapes off a thin layer of old skin, leaving you new. Able to feel the air, the shifting of the currents. Able to feel, more clearly than ever, the vibration of other people's feelings.

And there are other things you have learned. You know that Evie listens to the radio. Once, standing outside her door for a moment, you heard the sound of voices. You knocked and went in. As she said hello, she used her chin to touch one of the panel of buttons on her headboard and turn the radio off.

'You were in the middle of listening to something,' you said. 'Don't you want to hear the rest of it?'

She looked surprised.

'Good gracious, no.'

She settled her head back into the pillows.

'I listen to people speaking, the rise and fall of the voices. I am not very often interested in what they are saying. I don't listen to interviews or documentaries. I prefer plays and stories

I am not much concerned with what ordinary people think.'

She narrowed her eyes with good humour.

'I like the vibration of the human voice. Although perhaps not as much as I once did. There was a time, you know, when people on the radio were required to speak in a certain way. That has changed of course. Now it seems anyone can be on the radio, whatever their accent, and whether or not they have any sense of diction or modulation.'

Her own perfectly modulated voice is smooth and beautiful.

Another thing you have learned is that the roses around Evie's front door are yellow. That first day, they were dark, tight buds. You've watched them swell over the past month, the green calyx gradually losing its grip on the petals tucked inside. Today, you arrived to find the first of the flowers fully open. A harsh yellow, acidic, as though the long wait has jaundiced the petals. But they're pretty, with a nest of golden anthers sparkling in their middles.

The house has changed too since your first visit, become more detailed. There are three terracotta panels in the wall below the bay window. At first glance they are simply decorative, an elegant tapestry of leaves and flowers. But you have looked closely while waiting for Margaret Keyes to open the door.

In the left panel, a man stares open-mouthed at his own wrists, which are chained together.

In the middle panel there's a small monster, a dog-dragon, crouching between leaf and blossom, hissing.

The final panel hides a sleeping bat, upside down, its wings folded in sharp planes.

You wonder how many people over the years have admired the house and never noticed them. You wonder why they are there at all. A warning of evil ever present in the garden? A reminder of the dark within us all? You've become quite fond of them; they have revealed themselves to you. You wonder if Margaret has ever noticed them.

Unlikely. Too busy sulking.

You take a final swig of the thick tea and place it back on the little table.

'Do you believe your body has the power to punish you?' asks Evie. 'If you don't live a good life, do you think it's possible that your own body might rise against you, eventually, and make you pay for your wrongdoing?'

It's a question, but you aren't expected to answer. Some of Evie's questions do require an answer, of course. You're expected to open the box inside you where the truth lives, take it out, hang it up for her to consider. Sometimes it takes you a while to get the box fully open. Long minutes might pass while you finger its blank surfaces, looking for the seam, the crack that will let you in. You always find it eventually, and Evie always waits, her eyes steady and interested, as though the waiting is part of the answer.

Other times, Evie asks questions as an invitation to step onto some particular square on the map of her thoughts. The question is a signpost. *I am going here next. Would you like to come? To follow me you need to think in this direction...* When she is satisfied you are in the right place, she carries on with the exploration.

So now you consider the idea that your body could judge you, find you guilty, exact retribution. Was your body punishing you by being 'difficult' when you were younger? The possibility hovers, a humming winged thing that might settle, might find its home with you. But it moves on. No. If anything, your body had done you a favour – encouraged you to find something else to be, other than beautiful.

But there have been times, certainly, when your body has betrayed you. By feeling things it shouldn't. By not feeling things that it should. Your body obviously does not always have your best interests at heart.

'I believe it,' says Evie. So you refocus, bring her back into vision and watch her mouth closely as she shapes the words.

'I believe that my body is paying me back for all the bad things I've done in my life.'

It's hard to imagine that Evie has done anything bad. Not *that* bad. She's unkind to Margaret Keyes. But you understand now that Margaret Keyes has a lumpen petulance about her, a sullen peevishness, that could bring out the worst in anyone. You try to imagine being dependant on her for care and companionship, shrug the idea away.

'What have you done that could be that bad?' you ask.

She tightens her lips, makes deep lines of the fine wrinkles around her mouth.

'I want to tell you, Claire. I've wanted to talk about it for some time. It's not something I could speak about to just anyone, but it haunts me. And I am beginning to trust you. Yes, I'd like to tell you about it, if you're willing to listen.'

Something in you squirms with pleasure, uncoils in your stomach and begins to move upwards. It's too intimate to be seen, even by Evie; so you turn away before it reaches your face and move from the end of the bed to the window.

You can do that now. Move around the room; ask about this picture, that shawl. You've run the tips of your fingers across the carving on the marble fireplace, held the lush fabric of her old dresses against your cheek. The curtains are pearl-grey silk, they smell old and dry. The windows are clean on the inside, spotted on the outside. You wonder if Evie has a window cleaner, and whether she has the curtains drawn when he comes.

Beyond the glass, distorted by the watermarks, the garden is leathery. The ancient ivy has migrated in from the walls, hangs from the rhododendrons and convoluted apple trees. A dark oak looms in the far corner. There is no fresh growth, no blossom, although there are the remains of bluebells around the stone seat next to the pond. The strappy leaves hang over its edge, rotting into the murky water.

A small girl in a blue dress is standing there, looking up

towards your window. For an instant, you see yourself as she sees you – a narrow figure, serious, peering down at her from the dark terracotta wall. She smiles up at you and waves. But before you can wave back, she steps into the pond and lies back on the surface of the water, her hair spreading like a net. Then she sinks. For a few seconds she is a pale shape, face up just beneath the water, then she is too deep. You wait to see if she reappears, like Edward at the windmill. But the pond remains blank and dark.

'What's the worst thing *you've* ever done, Claire?' Evie's voice touches your back, rests between your shoulder blades.

'I thought you were going to tell me about *your* life...' you say, your eyes still on the pond.

'I am, my dear. I'm just thinking how to begin. Where to begin. It's surprisingly difficult to speak of these things, now I finally have the opportunity. Silly, isn't it?'

Turning to face her, you catch an unexpected shadow of vulnerability on her face. She looks soft, uncertain. This is something you haven't seen before.

Today, waiting to get off the train, you stood behind an old woman with soft white hair still clinging to the shape of the rollers, mild cotton wool sausages sitting above her pale neck. And you thought: Evie is old. But this is a different kind of old. This old lady is vulnerable. Fearful. Evie is like electricity. She can hardly move, but there's a spark about her. You thought: it's hard to imagine Evie frightened, ever.

Now you have seen something that makes Evie more accessible. Something that invites you to reciprocate.

'When I was sixteen,' you whisper, laying down as gently and as steadily on dangerous water as the little drowned girl, 'My mother tricked me into helping her commit suicide.'

Oh. There. After all this time.

Spoken aloud.

You wait a few beats, leaving space for Evie to react, expecting shock or disbelief. But Evie is simply listening. Frowning because she is concentrating, but you get the feeling Evie could believe anything. That Evie knows, how, in the right circumstances, anything is possible. Now she is simply waiting for you to tell her more.

'It was my job to give her a sleeping tablet at night. Every night.' You feel the ledge of the windowsill pressing into your back and you lean into it until it almost hurts. 'That last night, she distracted me. She made sure I forgot to move the bottle of tablets out of reach.'

Evie is still frowning.

'Are you absolutely certain that this is what happened?'

'I know she took all the tablets that night. I know she was dead the next morning.'

You breathe in through your nose, out through your mouth; there is no release in it; it is not a sigh.

'Sometimes I'm certain she distracted me deliberately. That she knew exactly what she was doing. Sometimes I think it just happened – and she just took her chance. Either way, she left me to bear it.' You want to keep your voice light, so you can keep going, but even you can hear how false it sounds. And Evie is not fooled by it.

'Help me understand completely, Claire,' she says. 'What did she leave you to bear?'

'That she did it without caring what it would be like for me afterwards. That she could use me like that.'

And something else.

'That I have to feel angry with her. All I wanted was to be able to feel sad when she died. That's not so much to ask, is it? To feel sad that your mother has died? But she made it so much more complicated.'

And more.

'She ruined it between me and Dad. He could never forgive me. She made absolutely sure that I never got close to him after she was gone.'

Evie hasn't even blinked.

'And you,' she says. 'Can you forgive yourself?' Her voice is soft.

But you haven't told her the worst part yet. The part that is unforgiveable. You can feel yourself sinking; this is too deep.

'The thing is – the really bad thing, Evie – is that when I was brushing my teeth, straight afterwards, I did remember.' You move back to the end of the bed, sit and look straight into her eyes so you can measure her reaction.

'I remembered that I'd left the tablets next to her by the bed, not on the shelf out of reach.

'I could have gone back and moved them. I should have done that.' You swallow the lump that is rising in your throat.

'But I didn't.'

Evie is silent. She doesn't look away, but she says nothing. You realize how grateful you are that she is not going to reassure you. She seems to understand what it has been to live with the weight of this.

'And it wasn't out of kindness,' you continue, determined to say it all. 'I didn't let it happen for her sake, because she couldn't bear her pain anymore. I let it happen because *I* couldn't bear her pain.'

You stop. You have to stop because your throat has constricted, as though your own body wants to stifle what is coming next. But the words come out. They are lifeless, but they come out.

'And maybe – I don't know if this is true – but maybe I did want my father all to myself. Maybe I wanted her to be gone, so he would finally see me.'

You are deep under the dark water now, looking up at the surface from below. Your words rise in slow bubbles, break through into the air.

And still Evie says nothing. And it's her silence, a thick rope of silence, that hauls you back, suddenly, above the water. The room is around you again. The smell of it. The colour and clutter. You take a deep breath.

'But he didn't see me. He never even spoke to me about what had happened. He moved out of the house as soon as I turned eighteen.' You notice that you have raised your hands, palms up, in front of you. (Empty, see?) You make them into fists and sit back down at the end of the bed.

'He lives by the sea now, in a flat with a balcony. We speak at Christmas and birthdays. He hasn't forgiven me yet. And I haven't forgiven her.'

Evie holds your gaze. You have never seen a kinder place than her eyes. You could fall into them. To stop that happening, you open your mouth and speak without thinking. And the question slips out easily, as though you were having an ordinary conversation.

'Do you ever think about dying?'

'Of course.'

'I often wonder how my mother knew, how she could be so sure, that she was ready to die. I mean, even in such pain, how could she know there weren't still going to be moments that were worth living for?'

Evie tilts her head in the way that means 'I'm thinking.'

'I don't know about your mother,' she says, eventually. 'I'll be ready to die when there's nothing to keep me entertained. When I'm finally ready to shut the door on my own thoughts and feelings. When I'm completely, irrevocably *bored* with the experience of being me, here.'

'But what if you were just having a bad day,' you say. 'What if you'd just waited a bit, and then felt better?'

'I couldn't agree more,' she says. 'I'm not suggesting doing anything impetuous.'

'And what about the people you'd leave behind? Don't they count?'

'At the end of the day, Claire, I doubt I could keep on living to meet someone else's need. That level of generosity just isn't in my nature.'

Evie's nature. That's what you had been going to talk about. Her nature. All the bad things she believes she's done in her life.

'I didn't mean to take so long to tell you my worse thing,' you say. 'And now we've run out of time. I have to cover for Martin this afternoon.'

'Not to worry,' she says, airy and bright. 'Next time.'

———

You select another length of honeysuckle, lay the stem along the ground, peg it down against the soil with a bent wire loop. You enjoy the comfortable squeeze of the wire into the earth and pat the stem flat, imagining how it might feel to be so sensitive to even the possibility of growth that just touching the earth would be a chance worth taking. And to take it, trusting that if you send out pale roots, there will be somewhere for them to go, something to attach to.

Another few loops and you're finished. You stand up, feeling the warm, damp patches at your knees where you have been kneeling. There has been so much rain over the past few weeks and so much sunshine. Everything is growing fast, you can almost see it happening in front of your eyes.

Your hands are filthy, the nails packed with dirt. You don't like wearing gloves, especially not for the fiddly jobs. So your hands are always dirty, there are always small scabs and scrapes. You wish the nails would stop growing; filing them is a chore, even the quick job you do after clipping them short. You will never have elegant hands.

You think about Evie's hands, about the way they rest on her stomach, curled into loose half fists. Evie should have elegant hands. They should be fine and slender. But although the fingers are long, they are blunt, the nails broad. Margaret Keyes must cut Evie's nails.

You see the two of them:

Margaret holding Evie's hand in hers, head bent close, filing with clumsy slow movements. Evie looking through her. Away from her. Refusing to be forced into intimacy.

You think about Evie's silver and turquoise rings. You think about Margaret sliding them onto her fingers.

You pick up another piece of wire and poke at the dirt under your thumbnail, cast an eye over your work, then use the secateurs to neaten the ends of the honeysuckle. Woodbine, it's called, when it's wild. Martin went through a phase when he knew everything about the folklore of plants. He told you woodbine was a sign of love. And that if you put it over your door it would keep out dangerous people and fevers, and other bad things.

Evie thinks bad things happen to bad people. She thinks her body is punishing her for bad things she has done. You like the idea that there is an inbuilt fairness to things; that people get what they deserve. But you're pretty sure the reality is a great deal more random than that.

As a survival strategy, being a good person is probably about as effective as putting honeysuckle over the door.

—

7

*T*his is what you have done:

Dismantled the bookshelves and dumped them outside
with the carpet and the dusty curtains. Soaked the wallpaper
with soapy water and scraped it off with a broad bladed wood
chisel. Cleared away the curls of wet paper that gathered in
drifts around the edges of the room, quickly, before they could
dry and stick to the floorboards.

Now the walls are bare. They are biscuit-coloured, seamed
and spotted with chalky white filler.

It didn't occur to you, as you were wiping down the skirting
boards and window frames, that you were washing away the
last traces of your parents. Now you notice: it's just a room, no
longer *their* room. The leather sofa, covered with a dustsheet,
is a soft island in the middle of an empty space.

Martin is whistling in the hallway. He misses a few notes
as he negotiates his way round the writing bureau, appears at
the doorway with two mugs of tea. He has chosen your mugs,
the chunky blue ones, not the white china teacups that were
your mother's.

'Nice kitchen,' he says, passing a mug to you, taking his
own to the window and leaning against the newly clean sill.

In all the years you've known him, Martin has never been
to the house. But he hasn't embarrassed you by making an

occasion of it. He hardly even raised his eyebrows when you asked him to come and help.

'Thanks for covering for me,' he'd said, arriving back at the nursery just as you were cashing up. 'I know you don't like being in the shop. Appreciate it.'

'That's okay.' Although it wasn't really okay. There was a knot of pain at the base of your neck, the muscles in your shoulders were clamped tight. Working in the shop is the one aspect of your job you really dislike. The low ceiling and tiny windows make it gloomy even on sunny days; it always smells sour and musty, of peat, fertiliser, dust. The products are packaged in bright primary colours. They shout.

You hate the niceties involved in serving people, the smiles and small talk. The last customer was a woman in outsized sunglasses who asked you to help load her stuff into a shiny four-wheel drive, then stood back and watched you do it on your own. The bag of compost split down the side as you heaved it into her boot, dark earth spilling out through the plastic.

Didn't do it on purpose.

Didn't tell her, either.

When it's quiet in the shop, part of the job is to work through the client list, phoning landscape gardeners and designers to promote the stock, the latest varieties of berberis or verbascum or French lavender. You had sat looking at the list for a long time, doodling a spider web in the corner of the page. You didn't call anyone.

'No, really,' Martin had insisted. 'I owe you one. What can I do to make it up to you?'

'You could help me redecorate the study,' you had said, as smoothly and evenly as if the idea had been waiting, clear and whole in your conscious mind – when in fact it had jumped straight out of your mouth, giving you no chance to edit, censor, ameliorate. And once spoken, the idea flapped in the air like a banner advertising your need. You wanted to reach out and pull it down.

'Sure. How about Sunday?' Martin said. 'Have you got the paint yet? I can pick some up on the way – what colour?'

'Just white. Thanks. Plain white.'

That was only last week. Just a few days ago. And now he is here, leaning against the window ledge, mug in one hand, gripped around the curve of the blue china rather than by the handle. Martin's hands are brown, his fingers as lean as the rest of him. His nails, like yours, are clipped short and worse for wear.

The tea is strong with not too much milk.

'Did you get the paint?' you ask.

'I certainly did.'

'Well,' you say, taking a sip of tea. 'That's good, then.'

Soon, Martin goes out to the van, comes back with a ten-litre tin. He pries open the lid with a screwdriver, tilts the tin so you can see. And it's not white. This colour hovers between pale green and blue. Soft. It glows in the tin.

'It's not white,' you say.

He grins at you.

'I thought white was a bit boring. Got them to mix this specially.'

'But I asked you to get white.'

I wanted *white*.

Didn't you hear me? Doesn't it matter what I want?

You take the in-breath, ready to speak. Then you see, in his face, that it does matter. The colour is a gift. So you exhale plain air instead of words.

'Do you like it?' he asks, still smiling.

You do. You love it.

'It's beautiful,' you say. 'Thank you, Martin. It's a beautiful colour.'

Soon, the two of you are covering the room in calm and

light, the paintbrushes making moist whisperings against the walls. The heat and the clean smell of emulsion surrounds you, lulls you.

'I've met someone recently,' you say. 'Someone really interesting. Different.'

Martin's paintbrush falls silent then. Your own continues unaccompanied, soft and wet, lapping at the wall. A lake of colour spreads out in front of you. You imagine yourself skimming across its surface, or floating, resting on its brightness. It would ripple gently, sounding like chimes, then settle around you.

'Who is it?'

His voice is low in the empty room, as though the top notes are lost, unable to find their way through the space between you. You turn to find him looking at you with serious eyes.

'Her name is Evie. I've been seeing her once a week. She's amazing, Martin. She lives in a huge old house in town and she can't move at all, or nearly at all. But she's incredible.'

You sneak a glance at Martin; he has lowered his chin, the way he does when he's going to argue.

'Really, Martin. I've never met anyone like her. It's as if she looks at things more closely than other people. I'm learning a lot. I think I'm even beginning to change some of things I don't like about myself.'

You realise you are starting to babble, and stop.

'You don't need to change,' Martin says. He is painting again, using slow extended strokes, pressing the paint hard out of the brush, making it stretch as far is will go.

'How do you know I don't need to change?'
'Well, I've known you long enough. What are you saying? That this woman has known you for a few weeks and suddenly she's an expert on what makes you tick?'

'You might not know me as well as you think you do.'

'Why? Because you don't *tell* me about yourself?' He laughs. 'I always know what you're thinking.'

'I doubt that very much.'

Even you can hear how precise and unfriendly your words sound. But Martin isn't frightened off.

'You give yourself away, Claire. Your expressions are dead easy to read. You say loads, all the time. You just don't say it out loud.'

You concentrate on keeping your face blank, focus on painting a straight edge along the skirting board while you weigh up your response. You know what has happened. You were touched by Martin's kindness about the colour. You gave something in return. Telling him about Evie had been your offering.

Why can't he just accept what's on offer?

Why does he have to push everything?

You feel your chest tightening, closing in on your heart and your breath. Your body is a step ahead of you, ready to defend against Martin's prodding.

I can just shut down.

But you hesitate, hovering on the threshold between open and closed. This isn't so very different to the times when Evie challenges you, and you survive those times; they leave you feeling raw but good.

Maybe you won't shut down.

Martin has resumed painting and is squinting, picking a hair from the paintbrush off the wall as he speaks.

'So what is this woman anyway, a counsellor or something? How come you've been going to see her every week?'

'It's part of my sentence,' you tell him, looking straight into his face. 'Community Punishment. I got caught shoplifting. I have to visit Evie every week. And I got a fine, too.'

Martin's face slackens with surprise.

You don't even try to disguise the ring of triumph in your voice.

'See? You don't know me that well after all, do you?'

—

As a child, you used to invent code. You made symbols out of solid dots and small circles, straight lines and squiggles. You simply replaced each letter of the alphabet with a different symbol. They would not have been difficult codes to crack. But it was magic, taking simple words and transforming them into something even you could not understand without referring to the key. You translated pages and pages into code. It felt significant to you, the rendering of familiar language into something strange. And it was important that only you knew how to unlock the meaning.

You showed a page to your mother.

'Can you read this?' you demanded.

She squinted and held it close to her eyes.

'I certainly can't,' she said.

'Good,' you said, and took back from her. 'Only I am supposed to know what it says.'

Sometimes, on the telephone in the shop, doodling in the margin of the order book, you find yourself drawing some of the code symbols from your childhood. It's remarkable, that you have brought these strange alphabets with you, accurate and unchanged.

———

Martin wants to know all about the shoplifting, the court case, the woman at the volunteer bureau. And you tell him, leaning heavily towards the facts rather than the feelings, placing your experiences in front of him like a row of stones. As the two of you finish painting, he listens, absorbs your words, puts a question here and there.

'What was going through your mind?' he asks. 'When you went into the shop – did you know you were going to steal something?'

Did you? Looking back, the clues were there. A particular kind of tension, even before you got to town. The uncomfortable feeling that your muscles and cells were paused somehow, like you were holding your breath. And then when you saw the scarf – or egg timer or ashtray or whatever it was – the recognition. That this was the thing you needed.

'I may have known,' you say, 'On some level. But not in my head; I didn't think about it beforehand. There was just a weird feeling of relief whenever I took something.'

'Then this wasn't the first time?'

You feel yourself shrinking inside. Ashamed.

'No. I've been doing it since my mum died. I just never got caught before.'

You want to look him in the eye, but you cannot lift your head.

When you were arrested, you had survived the shame of it by detaching, hovering above yourself so that what people said or thought didn't reach you. But now, here with Martin, you are not detached.

He is kneeling, wiping his brush off against the edge of the tin. Even in the late afternoon light, his hair is not auburn, or chestnut. It is just brown. The quiet, honest brown of riverbanks.

When he speaks, looking up at you as he presses the lid down, his voice is concerned, curious.

'Are you still doing it, Claire?'

'No. No I'm not.'

The magistrates had recommended a course of counselling. 'To help you deal with the emotions behind the shoplifting behaviour,' they said.

You said you would think about it.

'I haven't felt the need to do it again,' you tell Martin. And it's true. You haven't even thought about it.

'Maybe being caught cured me.'

Or maybe Evie did.

'It's a relief,' you say. 'To be rid of all those packages under the bed.'

They used to lurk there, pale and dusty. Now there is nothing under your bed.

'And it's a relief to be able to tell you about it,' you say, risking a quick glance to gauge his reaction. He smiles.

You see:

Yourself, turning into water,

Pouring into an earthenware bowl.

Resting there.

When the walls are done, the two of you lift the writing bureau back into the room, position it so it doesn't touch the nearly-dry paint, then load up the van with the remains of the shelves, the thin carpet, the old curtains. You heat up a tin of soup to share and bring it through to the living room.

Martin is kneeling in front of the low coffee table, scooping thick curls of butter onto a knife, spreading them onto crackers. You stir your soup. It's orange, not red, and shimmers in the white bowl. The deep round soupspoon is part of a set you inherited from your father's grandmother. They are not comfortable to use, too large, their edges almost sharp. But you like these spoons, their link to a different time, to a world of down-to-earth men and women who ate home made broth, not orange soup from a tin.

You are sitting with your legs tucked beneath you on the fat striped sofa in the living room. The door to the study is open, with the light on, so you can enjoy the new colour that shines through the doorway.

For a moment, you imagine Nanny Bee standing there, her big frame as familiar as ever. You wonder whether she would have liked the new colour. You wonder whether she would have liked Martin.

Yes. She would have liked Martin.

As if he senses your thoughts, Martin joins you on the sofa. He leans towards you, strokes your hair away from your face. 'Claire.'

'What?'

'You know.'

The part of you that feels most alive when Martin is around wants to bend towards him, pliant, like the soft new wood at the heart of the tree. But there is still the harder wood that surrounds it, and the shell of tough bark on the outside.

You run your own hand over your hair where he has touched it, making it yours again. Then you lean forward and put your empty orange-rimmed bowl on the coffee table.

'Martin, I wish you wouldn't.'

He sits back, regards you with steady eyes. They are not brown like your own eyes, like your parents' eyes and Evie's. Martin's eyes are light blue. It's not possible to look into them without seeing his otherness. He is another world, with a different sun, different air. You could get lost there.

You frown hard, feel your forehead wrinkle.

'I've known you a long time,' you say.

'Yes. And?'

'I've seen how it is with you. That things don't last.'

He raises his eyebrows in mock disbelief, but you go on.

'You've been telling me your secrets ever since we met, haven't you? So I know all about the women you've been involved with. It's always the same. They're special. They're the one you've been waiting for. Then they disappoint you.'

You swallow.

'I'd rather keep you as a friend.'

He puts his soup bowl down. 'And how can you be so sure it wouldn't be different with us?' he asks.

'How can you be sure it would?'

'You can't disappoint me,' he says, smiling.

You say nothing.

'Why do you always have to be so sensible?' Martin laughs. 'Doesn't your heart ever win? Don't you ever do anything without thinking about it?'

'No,' you say, calm now. 'I never do.'

When he's gone, the house settles back into silence, although you can still feel his presence. He has left trails of energy, like the tails of invisible comets. In the study, you are surrounded by Martin and by his vision of you: a woman who would love this amazing colour, who lives in it. You'll get a new carpet, something pale and soft. Maybe even some floaty transparent curtains. The electric light soaks into the walls, hums behind the newly painted surfaces. You can feel it even after you flick the switch and the room falls into darkness.

In the kitchen, you lean against the bleached wooden table and look around you. *Nice kitchen*, Martin had said. Hadn't commented on your gathered stuff, just acted like it's normal for people to cover every available space with twigs and stones. You scan the room from top to bottom, pretend you've never seen it before, make a point of noticing the details.

> Dark ceiling timbers, thready cobwebs. Shelves of crockery, none matching. Cupboards, handmade, with knocks and dents. Assorted wooden chairs, assorted vintage cushions. Red quarry tile floor, grubby.

And overall, it does feel nice. Unpretentious and comfortable. It's also undeniably tatty. Except for the new fridge – a shiny white fridge with perfect corners and a silver handle.

When the men came to take the old fridge away, they weren't rude, but they were loud. One older, one younger, both in dirty jeans and T-shirts. They brought their roughness into the kitchen, spoke to you with too much familiarity. And you had made yourself cheerful and pleasant, smiled and thanked them. Then you shut the door and felt grateful for the quiet that settled back over the room.

The old fridge used to sit humming crazy things to itself in the space between the cupboard and the sink. Now there was a square of thick dust on the floor there. You dragged the brush towards the dustpan and dust had tumbled in the air like ash. You prodded in the space between the cupboard and the skirting board, and it gave up years' worth of debris: unrecognisable shrivelled things and balls of greasy fluff – and a small grey square of paper. A till slip? A note? It was folded into four.

Back at the table, wood solid under your elbows, you smoothed out the folded paper and your father's sharp, tight handwriting had spooled out in front of you:

Matches. Soap. Onions. Potatoes. White vinegar.

White vinegar for your mother. Just a small amount mixed with water.

See:

> *Your father soaking the facecloth, leaning over her, crane-like, his soft black hair falling in a block over his forehead. He dabs her face carefully, avoiding her eyes.*

> *'Doesn't it sting, Mum?' you ask from the doorway. You don't like to go into her room. Not just because it's a sick room, not just because your mother's painful breathing has turned the air dry and sour. You don't like to go in because it feels like intruding.*

> *'No, it's good,' she says in the new voice – the coarse, deep voice that has taken over in the past few weeks. 'Helps me breathe… clears my head.'*

> *But then she coughs. Your father soaks the cloth again, wrings it out, lays it on her forehead.*

> *He makes a sound then, his head dips. She reaches up and touches his face.*

> *You turn away.*

For years, the thin grey square of paper had waited there behind the fridge, carrying the memory like a packet to be delivered. You had rested your fingertips on your father's handwriting, feeling for a trace of him in the ink.

———

Washing the mugs and soup bowls, you think: of course Martin feels threatened by Evie. There's never been anyone else; not that he's known about. You've never mentioned the brief comings and goings of others; they have never encroached, never changed the lie of the land between the two of you. Now here's Evie, occupying space, altering the horizon, casting new shadows.

Martin will have to adjust, take Evie into account like a new landmark. You slide into his viewpoint then back into your own. It throws you off balance. Like standing on the shingle at the edge of the sea – that sucking, shifting feeling under your feet as the water recedes.

You wonder if you have told him too much. You said: *I'd rather keep you as a friend.* You didn't say: *rather than a lover who will disappoint you and lose you.* He knew you meant that.

Friend. It's what people can become if you tell them about yourself; if they listen; if they absorb the things you say. You imagine your words entering Martin's bloodstream, swimming there, being broken down, incorporated into his flesh.

You dry the mugs, put them back on their hooks, notice how hot it is, how sticky you feel.

You wish it would rain.

———

8

The real library would be organised and quiet. This is the temporary library – everything crammed into one floor in an office block while the real library is being refurbished. Noisy, busy, small. The air is stale and hot.

The librarian who showed you where to look was a mild man in a tailored shirt, cuffs neatly folded back, fingernails neatly tended. He led the way to the psychology section – clinical psychology, not popular psychology – pointed at the shelf and left you to it.

You run your forefinger along the spines of the shelved books, feeling the rise and fall of the covers. This is the gathered wisdom and disorder of many minds. You choose a diagnostic manual and sit on the floor against the wall, the heavy book open on your knees, your notebook and pen on the grey carpet tiled floor beside you.

Psychosomatic. It means:

Related to a disorder that has physical symptoms but is caused by mental or emotional factors.

Concerned with the relationship between the mind and the body.

The word wasn't in your father's dictionary. That had offered *bedridden* (confined to bed because of illness or infirmity). But that had not been enough.

You lean back, feeling the wall press against your shoulders, and close your eyes. The heat and hum of voices flows over you. You take a deep breath, feel warm air in your nostrils, the rising of your chest. Exhaling, the lowering of your rib cage. The pause between breaths is long and peaceful. You pay attention to what your body tells you – the floor beneath you is hard; a draft of warm air is stroking the left side of your face; your stomach gurgles; you feel hunger; the edge of the book is pressing into your thighs.

Then you change focus and listen to the whispering of your mind:

> is anyone looking at me do they think I'm weird on the floor with my eyes closed there's a sandwich in my rucksack in the car it's so hot I should open my eyes

You open your eyes, glance back at the page in front of you. *The relationship between the mind and the body.*

> Like in a family: you don't get to choose it and you can't escape it.

This is not a reassuring thought. You consider the possibilities.

If the mind is in charge, like a train driver, you can only hope it will be vigilant and keep your body safely on track. You can hope it will be wise and make good, caring choices. And you can hope your body will do what it's told.

You raise your hand, consider the shapes and lines in your palm, wiggle each finger in turn, then all of them at once.

But what if the mind isn't a separate thing, sitting up there in the top of your head? What if it's woven into all your cells and nerves from head to foot? Mind and body might work together, decide together: *given the circumstances, this is the best course of action.*

Is this the agreement Evie's mind and body have made? To stop moving in her own best interests?

Back in the book, there's more.

Pseudoparalysis:

Extreme loss of muscle strength and control, not true paralysis.

Conversion disorder:

Numbness and paralysis without neurological explanation.

Repressed emotion converted into physical symptoms.

You write it all down.

———

9

Evie asks:

'Do you have any friends, Claire? I mean, apart from the friendship that is developing between the two of us –' *you enjoy a warm trickle of self-satisfaction* '– who else is there in your life?'

You tell her about Martin. About the pull to be closer, the need to be careful. About the sense that something might be changing.

'I think,' you tell her, 'That my friendship with you might be helping me dare to risk a bit more with Martin.'

Evie smiles softly. 'That is lovely to hear. I remember the prickly young woman who first came to see me. Who could have predicted that you would let down your guard to such an extent? And what a sweet, sensitive heart you have been protecting.'

You lean back against the footboard, feeling languid, a sense of wellbeing soft in you like honey.

'And that,' says Evie, suddenly grave. 'Is why it's so important that you don't rush, my dear. Open yourself to new closeness, by all means. But take it slowly. You need to be sure you can trust your Martin to treat you gently.'

Evie shakes her head, slowly, in tiny increments. 'I know from experience how hard it can be when a close friend lets you down.'

This is surprising. You are so used to seeing Evie as alone in the world. You have assumed you are her only regular visitor; now you cringe at your own presumption. Of course she has had close friendships. Perhaps even still does.

'Do you have a best friend, Evie?'

'I did. I had a friend who made everything special. Grace. Her name was Grace Cullen. I have never been closer to anyone.'

You feel a spurt of jealousy.

'And now?' you ask.

'Now,' she twinkles. 'There is no-one closer than you, my dear.'

You are soothed.

She says: 'Could you get that photograph for me? The one in the silver frame?'

It is a black and white photograph: a toddler in a white dress and satin shoes. She is propped next to a vase of flowers like an ornament; unaware of the camera, intent on one of the lilies in the vase. Her cheeks are plump, her dark hair curly.

You hold the photo up for Evie, put it on the table next to her bed where she can see it.

'Goodness, I haven't looked at this for a very long time. I still have that little christening dress, you know, in a box in the attic. But I have no recollection of being this little person on this day, of sitting next to the flowers and having my photograph taken. I suppose the memory must be somewhere in me, though, buried beneath a million more recent events.'

She studies the photograph closely, as if it might unlock the memory. Then she looks up at you.

'I believe that, Claire. That we keep all our memories. And when we can't remember something, it's a problem of access rather than storage. Amazing, isn't it, to think we have our whole lives, moment by moment, hoarded away in our brains?'

You nod. 'Wouldn't it be incredible,' you venture, 'If we

could just go and look at them when we wanted, like a film...'

Evie turns back to the photo.

'Looking at this,' she continues as if you haven't spoken, 'There's no clue – nothing in this small child's expression or features – as to the kind of person I would become. Perhaps that's true of most people, my dear, do you think?'

This time you wait to see whether a response is required. It isn't. She continues:

'Although it seems to me that there are certain children who spring from the womb ready-made, their personalities already intact. And then it is simply a question of watching them grow into larger versions of themselves. Or perhaps,' she tilts her head as she considers the thought, 'Perhaps it's just that such children are born with their characters very close to the surface, showing from the start, whilst others must be revealed gradually.'

She pauses.

'Then again, some people claim, I'm sure you know, that we are a blank canvas at birth, without personality until life creates one for us.'

She looks at you, seems to realise that you are hovering. 'Do sit down Claire, you'll be more comfortable.' So you sit in the brocade chair at the foot of the bed.

She closes her eyes. You watch her face as she speaks.

'Freud wrote quite a lot about it, of course. How children develop into adults. As I understand it, he suggested that very small children go through a phase of sexual awareness. You may be familiar with this idea, Claire.'

Her eyes remain closed. You mumble yes very quietly, to let her know you are still listening, although you are not sure this is necessary.

She opens her eyes again, they are darker than you have ever seen them.

'It's alright, Claire. If I want your input I will ask for it. Just relax and listen. Would you do that for me?'

'Yes,' you say again. She closes her eyes; resumes:

'During this time,' she says, 'Children are little bundles of sexual energy, their nerve endings alive with pleasure. Then, according to Freud, they simply forget about all that. Having made decisions, unconsciously, that will determine who they become, they enter into a phase of sexual dormancy that lasts until puberty.'

Evie's eyes remain shut as she speaks; her eyelids flicker as though she is watching the story unfold behind them. This is strange. Like receiving a confession. It seems wrong, intrusive, to watch her face as she speaks. So you close your own eyes. And then there is nothing but Evie's words and the pictures they evoke behind your own eyelids.

'For the life of me,' she says, her voice fluid. 'I can't imagine why any living being would just forget about anything that felt that good! Certainly, the small child that I grew out of never forgot. She learned it felt good to rub herself and even better to wriggle and rub against another body. Any body.'

You see:

> *Round children, water babies, squealing as they tumble naked together.*

You find yourself holding your breath. Evie seems to sense this; she says:

'No, this is not shocking, Claire. This is nothing to be embarrassed about. It was all entirely natural; it was about pleasure, not sex. The little girl would wrap her arms around her mother's neck and fold herself into her mother's body and melt. Or tuck her face into her father's throat and lick his skin.

'Apparently, most children grow out of this kind of behaviour when they're five or six, but this little girl didn't grow out of it then. Eventually her mother began to push her away. This is what adults need to do. Set limits. Her mother knew this. But her father did not.

'She's just affectionate,' he would say. 'She's sweet.'

'And that was how she first began to learn about a certain kind of power. When she sat on her father's lap – when she wouldn't get down and he wouldn't make her – and her mother's jaw would get tight.'

'Don't squirm, Evie. Sit still,' her mother would say with hard eyes.

'She's alright,' her father would say.

'Now that's interesting, isn't it? According to the experts, parents should present their children with a united front. But I wonder what that little girl would have learned if her parents had agreed about how much intimacy was appropriate? She found it such a valuable asset, to know her own power. And how else might she have learned it, do you think?

'Her parents didn't argue though. They never argued. Her mother simply acquiesced, in every instance, without comment. But you must know, my dear, that people have many ways of communicating their feelings that don't involve words. In my mother's case, disapproval was like a dry smell that followed her wherever she went. And it was precisely because she disapproved of so much that it was so easy to ignore her. I aligned myself with my father, knowing she would retreat.

'Of course, when he wasn't around, I paid the price. She could be a spiteful woman.

'Looking back now, I can see that she was unhappy. And I must have known that as a child, but I didn't care. I must have learned from my father, very early on, that my mother simply wasn't very important. She talked constantly, under her breath, about whatever she was doing, about the weather, about the goings on of the neighbours. But her voice was like the music they play in supermarkets. Most of the time, I simply didn't hear her.

'I noticed everything about my father, though. He smelled like engine oil. A syrupy, bitter smell. In the winter, I had to hunt for it, sniffing at his clothes like a terrier. In the summer months, it followed him in wafts. His hands were covered in tiny seams of black, where the oil had seeped into the cracks and creases of his knuckles and the skin around his fingernails. His hands were very hard and his fingers were blunt. I used to wonder whether he could still feel things when he touched them.

'When I was small, my father's differentness fascinated me. I liked the coarseness of the fabric in his overalls and the roughness of his face. I liked the sharpness of his jaw and elbows and the sudden hard direction of his movements. That he smoked. That he spoke rarely and used few words when he did.

'It was only when I grew older that I noticed his teeth were stained brown and the arms and back of his chair were marked with oily patches. I noticed that when he spoke, it was only ever to make statements or demands, that he didn't listen.

'He was like one of those photographs that develops in front of your eyes – the detail and shape and the colour gradually become clear until you can see what is there. And then it stops developing, stays the same, nothing changes after that.

'But my mother never seemed to develop at all. She was always the same. Hard and disappointed. Except, for a while, after my brother was born. I watched her soften and shine then and I wondered whether she had once been like that with me. I watched to see how long it would last; whether the shine would wear off. And it did.

'I loved my new brother. His small body was completely defenceless against my love, you see. I could hold him and stroke him and rub my cheek against the fine hair on his head, and touch him where I wanted to, as long as my mother wasn't watching. I could fill myself up with the kind of contact I craved. It was wonderful. Naturally, as he grew older, less so. And then I lost him altogether.

'Of course, the sense of loss went away, with time. Everything does, you know, eventually. Everything passes.'

Evie sighs and is silent for a long minute. Then, without opening her eyes, she says:

'That's enough now, my dear. I'm tired.'

—

On your way back to the station, you feel the corners of your mouth pulling slightly and realize you are smiling as you walk. Evie is telling you her story. A story she has never shared with anyone before. The sense of satisfaction is delicious, thick and heavy, like cream. And yet, some of what she has told you was not comfortable to hear, is not comfortable to carry with you. You see:

> *A small girl squirming on her father's lap, then lying back, resting against his chest. She sings to him, a tuneless nonsense song about her daddy, while her brown eyes follow her mother moving about the room.*

The train is early. You sit in the window, washed in the warmth of the glassy sunlight, waiting for the carriages to move off. The seat vibrates beneath you; the window buzzes gently against your cheek.

—

10

In the seconds between sleep and waking, you find yourself face down on a raft on a lake. The grey wooden planks of the raft are warm under your stomach, smooth and soft. You can hear the gentle suck of the water below, feel the liquid cushion of it. The sun is warm on your back. You are leaning over the edge of the raft, pressing a big glass bowl against the surface of the water, making a curved window into the lake. You lean further, your face pressed into the bowl, eyes adjusting to the dark of the underwater.

And then the perspective shifts: you are looking down from a high place at your own body on the square of raft. From here, you can see there are no edges to the lake; it goes on forever. You can see that there is cause for concern, the raft is tiny, could be so easily lost. And then you are higher still and cannot make out the figure on the raft, or the raft. There is just the lake.

And then you take a breath, and open your eyes, and forget.

———

'How do you know so much about psychology? About Freud and the way children develop?' Today, you are sitting in the chair at the foot of Evie's bed: chocolate brown brocade and velvet cushions with turquoise tassels. Your shoes off, both your legs are tucked over one arm of the chair.

'Did you study it?' you ask.

'In a manner of speaking,' she says. 'Not in any formal way, but yes, I made it my business to read, to learn. I have always felt the need to understand how people work, what shapes them. And how they can be shaped.' She looks up at you from under arched brows and smiles.

You smile back, dangling your feet, flexing your toes in your socks.

'Something else I was wondering,' you say. 'What happened with your brother? Why did it suddenly end?'

Evie closes her eyes and keeps them closed for so long that you wonder whether she will open them again. And then she does.

'My mother took him away,' she says. 'We woke one day and she was gone, and he with her.'

'Leaving you alone with your father?'

'Yes. And you'd think, wouldn't you, that he would have been fine about seeing her gone. He had, after all, always treated her with such indifference. But he was devastated. He became silent, ate little, drank a lot. I was very glad, in the end, to be able to leave.'

'When did you leave?' you ask. 'Where did you go?'

Evie shakes her head. 'My dear, that is a story for another time. But I'm delighted to know that you are interested. Thank you for listening with such attention. And now,' she looks mischievous, 'Tell me about you. What's been happening between you and your friend Martin since we last spoke?'

Darling Claire,

I was just lying here, drifting, and the strangest thing popped into my head. I remembered that you had an imaginary friend when you were little. A tall lady in a flowered dress. You told us about her almost as soon as you could talk and you were convinced she lived here with us. It was very sweet – you would describe what she was doing as if you really could see her.

We discussed it, your father and I. He liked the fact that you were using your imagination, he saw it as a sign of creativity. I was worried; it seemed introverted to me, and very strange. In the end, we decided to let it run its course, but without encouraging it, or playing along.

The next time you mentioned her, I told you we couldn't see her. You seemed quite astonished. I think you thought there was something wrong with us! I remember your little face, so serious and puzzled. But in the end, you stopped talking about her. I guess you just grew out of it, as children do. You've probably forgotten all about it.

Isn't it funny, the things we remember when we have nothing else to do?

You don't remember telling your parents about Nanny Bee. But you can remember feeling confused when you realised they couldn't see her, as if they might be playing a joke together. Until you read this letter, you had no idea that your relationship with Nanny Bee had been a cause for concern or discussion but you like the idea that your father saw Nanny Bee as evidence of your creativity. You wonder how he'd feel if he knew you still see people who aren't really there. Lots of them.

Maybe I am imagining them all.

Maybe I am truly insane.

The thought has no energy at all. It slides away easily, has no barbs, because it is simply not true. You know, with absolute certainty, that the dead people you see are real.

So why not tell Evie?

Now that's a thought. The ghosts are your deepest secret.

More secret even than the night your mother died. What would it be like to share them with Evie? Being the sole witness to their sadness, their indifference, can be hard to bear. It might be a relief to share the weight of that, to let go of that aloneness. It might be like resting. You feel yourself hovering, testing the possibility. And then you settle.

One day.

But not yet.

———

11

The rhythmic clickety-clack associated with trains doesn't really exist; it's a figment of the collective imagination. Sometimes the train achieves a kind of almost-rhythm, but there is too much stopping and starting, too many variations in speed. You can feel yourself willing it to find a pattern. You are frustrated by each missed beat. The only way to cope is to actively not care whether the train achieves a rhythm or not. You can read. You can watch things out the window. You can ignore your body's call for a regular pulse, your heart crying out for a mirror to its own beating.

You prefer to get the train when you visit Evie so you don't arive keyed up from the drive. The train carries you from the single airy platform in the village, empty, with just a machine for tickets, to the station in town, the busy welcome of warm concrete and oil stains and digital clocks that count the seconds in audible clicks.

It has become a ritual, this journey to Evie. From the moment you step onto the village platform you feel connected to her. That sense of connection will carry you safely off the train at the other end, through the crowds at the station. And as you walk down the Avenue, you will feel that link growing stronger, a kind of excitement that is not very different to anxiety.

Today, you are sharing the carriage with a young family. A

woman, her husband, two children. She is thin and hard. They are soft and pasty. The tattooed man is not in your carriage today.

The first time you saw him, he was asleep in the seat opposite you. His closed eyelids were pale blue, lighter than the rest of his face. You could see the soft small domes of his corneas under the thin skin. His head rocked gently against the headrest with the movement of the train. On the curve of his left cheekbone, its scales etched in blueblack: a small lizard, as accurate as the line drawings in your father's dictionary. It is real enough, resting along the angle of his face, that you could imagine it darting into his hairline.

On his neck: a compass, the kind you see on very old maps. The N for North is large and curling, the other points are arrows. There is something else that disappears into the grey of his shirt – the tip of a feather or a spray of water at the base of his throat. The skin is dark there, the stubble just under the skin.

When the man swallowed, his Adam's Apple moved and you had looked up from his throat to find his eyes open, an unsettling pale green, expressionless. Embarrassed, you wanted to look away, but that seemed rude too. Then the wrinkles around his eyes deepened, his eyes narrowed. He was smiling. A warm smile, as simple to receive as the smile of a child. But before your mouth could shape a smile of your own to return, he had faded into the blue weave of the seat and was gone.

You've seen him many times since. Always in the same compartment, in a seat by a window. Sometimes he sleeps the whole way through, sometimes he is already awake when you get on the train; he watches the countryside rattle by. Now you don't stare and he doesn't smile. Often, you don't even notice when he fades away. He is always gone by the time you get off at your stop.

———

'What is your most treasured possession?' asks Evie.

You are at her mantelpiece, looking closely at a carved figurine, a dancing goddess, smooth and fragile in red wood. You put it down and move to the foot of Evie's bed.

'I'm not sure I have a most treasured possession,' you say. 'I'm not really that interested in material things. But I like collecting seed pods and bits of wood when I go for walks.'

A branch stripped of its bark.

A plait of ivy root.

A spray of bracken, dull orange.

Sharp stones that glint when they catch the light.

Flat smooth stones the colour of clay or oatmeal.

A chestnut.

'I like arranging them in patterns, but I wouldn't call them possessions. Sometimes I just arrange them in the woods where I find them. I like the idea of someone coming across them, being surprised by them. But I also like the idea of them remaining unfound. Just settling into the earth, falling apart on their own.'

You fiddle with the tassel on a cushion, combing its tangled silk threads with your fingers.

'Sometimes I take things home and put them in vases for a while. My kitchen table is covered with jars full of dry sticks and piles of seedheads and pebbles. But I put them out in the garden after a while. I collect things and let them go. I don't think I have a most treasured possession.'

Evie ponders.

'Don't consider it in material terms, then. If your house were on fire, which of the things within it would you most want to rescue?'

'Oh.'

You see:

The white house, smoke billowing from the windows.

You fling open the door, hold your hand over mouth and nose, make your way through the stink of burning and the awful crackling of flames into the study to the writing bureau. Eyes streaming, face tight with heat, you grab the box containing your mother's letters and the dictionary your father gave you. Holding them to your chest, you stumble back through the smoke-filled kitchen and out of the door, gasping.

Behind you, the roof collapses in sparks.

'My mother's letters. My father's dictionary,' you tell Evie.

She looks alert, like a bird that has sensed a worm and is listening for the vibrations that will give away its location.

'Haven't I told you about my mother's letters?' you ask.

'I don't believe you have,' she says. And waits.

So you tell her.

'What kind of thing did she write about?' Evie wants to know.

'Just what she was thinking and feeling at the time. Things she remembered about being my mother. Things she thought about me. That kind of thing.'

You lean back in the chair, press your spine flat.

'I think she had a romantic idea about what it was to be a dying mother.'

'Do you still read them?'

'Occasionally. It's not what she says that's important. Not like real wisdom or guidance.'

'It just gives you something to think about,' Evie completes your thought. 'A theme or an idea to consider against the context of your life.'

'Yes. Exactly that.' And it's like Evie has reached out her hand and touched yours. You can almost feel the small weight of it.

'Do you have a most treasured possession?' you ask.

She smiles and nods to indicate the cluttered room.

'As you can see my dear, I do have a passion for things. Or at least I did. But there's no single thing that I value most highly. For me, the delight is in owning all of it. It isn't enough to possess just one thing. So I too am a collector. But I don't let go of anything, ever.'

She twinkles at you. Her voice is confiding.

'I wonder what modern psychiatry would make of us, my dear? You unable to keep anything, me unwilling to let anything go. Perhaps I am simply greedy. As soon as I own a thing, as soon as it's mine, I want the next thing.'

'So if your house was on fire,' you say, 'What would you want to rescue?'

'If this house caught fire,' Evie laughs. 'Everything would be burnt to a crisp. Myself included, no doubt.'

———

You are taking an inventory of the clutter on your kitchen table.

A stone shaped like a whale, rounded and smooth. You spotted it half buried in the path; you worked the earth away with your fingertips to release it, found it just as smooth and grey on the other side.

A naked branch. The bark has peeled away, leaving pale wood that shines like bone or antler. You wonder if, somewhere in the woods, there might be a matching husk of bark like a discarded snakeskin.

A leaf skeleton. The green flesh of the leaf has decayed perfectly, leaving the lacework of veins intact.

Each of these has been collected for a reason. There is nothing random about gathering, just as there was nothing random about taking things from shops. In each case, you recognised the thing you needed.

This is not the same as acquiring things simply because you want them. Evie's things are acquired. She has no emotional connection to individual items; she relates to the sum of the things she owns. It doesn't matter how exquisite an object, how beautifully crafted. She spends every hour of every day surrounded by wonderful things. You doubt she even notices them.

See:

> *The room is silent, except for the ticking of the clock. Evie is alone, propped up against the vibrant pillows. Only her eyes move, wander around the room, resting briefly here and there on the objects that fill the space. Nothing holds her attention. For long minutes, she simply stares at the ceiling. Then she turns her head to touch the button that will turn on her radio.*

> *Margaret has moved it; it is just out of reach.*

You pick up a sponge, rinse it under the tap and wipe the counter in gently widening circles, as if you are wiping mist off a window.

Evie has implied that Margaret can be spiteful, but you're not sure exactly what that means. The first time she mentioned it, you had been looking at a pair of her gloves, one of many you found in a satin hatbox on the floor next to the massive wardrobe. These were deep blue, elbow length. Too delicate for you to even consider inserting your own hand.

'My dear could you move my arm, please? It is resting badly. If you could just straighten it a little?'

You put the gloves back in the box, took the few steps over to Evie's bed. You felt breathless, nervous; you had never touched Evie before. She watched with calm eyes as you slipped your hands under her arm – one above the elbow, one above the wrist. You could feel her skin, warm through the lavender silk of her tunic, the softness of her flesh. Tentative, you lifted, and the arm was heavier than you expected. And it wasn't stiff; it bent at the elbow as you raised it, so you readjusted the position of your hands and tried again, shifting Evie's arm carefully, replacing it lightly on the bed. You stroked her sleeve back into place. Patted. When you looked at her face again she was smiling.

'Thank you, Claire, that was very kind and wonderfully gentle. I am not used to it.' Her smile became lopsided as she frowned. 'Margaret Keyes is not the gentlest of creatures, you know. She's naturally clumsy, of course, and I suspect she can't help that. But I do wonder whether her hands are harder, her brush strokes sharper, because she is at heart such a resentful woman.'

'She hurts you?' You felt a flush of warmth rising in your chest: anger. 'Evie, are you saying that Margaret hurts you?'

'No, my dear. Not really.' Evie took a breath and seemed about to say more. But then there was a knock at the door and Margaret came in with the tea and lemon juice. You watched as she moved awkwardly through the abrupt silence, not looking either of you in the face, depositing the tea on your side table, the juice on Evie's, then shuffling out. And Evie had pressed her lips together, wouldn't say any more about it.

Now you wonder how far Margaret's spitefulness really goes. A lump of anxiety swells in your stomach. You think about stories you have heard about abuse that has gone unchecked, about neighbours who lacked the confidence to intervene. Margaret is sullen, capable of malice. Nothing more, surely.

You can never be sure, even about people close to you.

Who knows?

You think about Evie's mother, a pushover for so many years, entirely predictable, who suddenly surprised everyone.

You rinse the sponge, squeeze the water out, throw it into the sink. Then you choose a few of the objects on the kitchen table, put them outside the back door. A small wicker dish full of acorns. A bunch of dusty bracken fronds. A slice of oak, flat and round.

You will take them into the woods next time you go, and leave them there.

———

– *12* –

Evie says:

'I had no idea, until I started school, that I was bright. My parents didn't read, not for pleasure. There were very few books in our house.

'In our house, the radio was always on. And later, when we got one, the television. Sometimes both at the same time. Not loud enough to be able to hear properly, just loud enough to fill the space and make it difficult for people to talk to one another.

'People are still debating, aren't they, about the impact of television? Still questioning how much of an influence it has, whether it really can shape people's thoughts and actions. I find it astonishing that there's any doubt. People are infinitely malleable, my dear. They can be bullied or cajoled into just about anything, often without even noticing it's happening. How could they fail to be influenced by the images and ideas that come into their own homes?

'As a child, the radio and the television had a profound impact on me. They showed me there were other ways to live. Other places, where people lived in houses that didn't all look exactly the same, children did not play in the street, where neighbours did not shout from one doorway to the next. Where men wore suits to work, where women wore beautiful clothes and had jobs too. These lives were littered with lovely things, perfumes and skin care products, candles at dinnertime. The people who lived these lives ate in restaurants, and drank wine with their meals, even at home. Their gardens were full of flowering shrubs and elegant garden furniture.

'But more than anything, the people who lived so differently to us also spoke differently. Quietly, with authority. They didn't shout as a matter of course or use swear words casually, like punctuation. Their voices were measured, as if they were worth something.

'I wanted to speak like that. I wanted another life, so I needed to speak like that.

'I had a small radio. I listened, constantly, to the BBC. I practised speaking the way presenters spoke. Over and over, in my bed at night, I recited the shipping forecast. Repeated the news. I memorised phrases that women used in interviews.

'In time, I had two different voices. One for my family and people who knew me. The other for when I was out on my own, amongst strangers. It was a considered voice, a bit deeper than my natural voice, slower and clearer.

'What surprises me, still, as I look back, is that I was so ready to judge the world I lived in. And I did judge it, very harshly indeed. I was eleven years old and I despised my parents.'

Evie opens her eyes. 'Really. I was furious with the life I had been given. But where did I get the idea that I had been short-changed? That the world owed me a living? So many people didn't appreciate what they had. It seemed such a waste. I deserved it more.'

She looks up at you from under arched brows.

'I think, Claire, that you are someone who appreciates things?'

You nod uncertainly.

'I have seen how you consider the things in this room,' she says. 'Do you like this house?'

'I love this house,' you say without hesitation.

And you realize it's true. You feel accepted here. The

house, once forbidding, is revealing itself to you, bit by bit.

'That's what a house like this needs,' says Evie. 'It's an extraordinary house. I can't bear to think that when I am gone, it will go to someone who doesn't appreciate it. Even worse, that it could be divided into flats, lose its integrity.'

She looks intently at you, her eyes like liquid.

'Perhaps I will leave it to you in my Will.' She smiles. 'You would rattle around in it like a pea in a pod, but I could trust you to care for it, couldn't I?'

You don't reply. It's not always easy to tell when Evie is joking. But she can't possibly be serious about leaving her house to you.

Can she?

Evie makes her own rules.

———

On the train, there is a blonde girl in a school uniform; she is listening to music through earphones. You can hear the high notes buzzing around her head.

You close your eyes, see:

Another girl, dark and intense, sitting on a single bed; her back is against the wall, her legs folded up against her chest. The small radio is balanced on her knees.

She listens, head tilted towards the speaker.

She repeats the words to herself, mouthing them silently.

She turns the volume down and says them again out loud. Quietly, so her parents will not hear.

———

13

There is something about the sound of woodpigeons. It always soothes you, takes you to a place inside yourself that is peaceful. You are surprised it even exists, this peaceful place, cannot remember how it came to be. But the sound of a woodpigeon calling is like a gift. A tremulous gift of sound like a balm. You see:

> *Yourself, lying on a blanket on the ground in the gentle sun, half asleep, half awake.*

> *Your father, sitting in a deckchair a few feet away, reading aloud to your mother.*

> *His words are fuzzy; they float around her, a swarm of slow attentive bees. And in the tree above them, a woodpigeon calls, the long notes punctuating your father's measured sentences like strange music.*

Today, a woodpigeon is calling across the churchyard from the top of the yew tree. It has been a long time since you came here. Years. You are wary of nostalgia; only a shade away from grief, it can tip so easily into something that hurts. But today the memories are kind, the gravestones are old friends. Moving amongst them, you remember the names, recognise the patterns of the words.

> Sacred to the memory of Mary, daughter of William and Sally Miller

You used to challenge yourself to remember who was buried where. You would sit under the yew, close your eyes and think of a name. Then you had to jump up and walk straight to the correct gravestone, at a steady pace, not allowing yourself to look left or right for clues.

> To the memory of Elizabeth, amiable daughter of Mr. Joseph and Celia Buxton

Somehow, you have always known that none of the graves here belongs to Nanny Bee. It would make sense for her to have lived nearby, died nearby, and been buried in this churchyard. You would recognise Nanny Bee's grave if you ever saw it, you are certain.

> In loving memory of Thomas Finch, died April 9th 1909 aged 71 years

You still have no idea how Nanny Bee was connected to the white house that once belonged to the vicar, or why she left. You don't like the idea of strong, independent Nanny Bee being forced to do anything against her will. You would rather she had her own reasons for going, even though it hurts to think she'd chosen to leave you.

At the yew tree, you press your palm against the rough bark of the trunk. It feels dry and quiet, you get no sense of the sap moving through it. Perhaps it lives more slowly than other trees. Perhaps you would have to slow your own breathing and heartbeat in order to detect it. You wonder if Nanny Bee had been as sad to leave as you were to lose her.

Next to the fence, there is a clump of dry thistles, grey and silver, the ghosts of last season. You snap the thistleheads off one by one, consider gathering them into a small pile like a cairn to mark the way. But they are dry and light. It will not take much to scatter them. Instead, you let them fall from your hands, and go sit in the soft grass where you can lean back against James Frank Strong. The late afternoon sun is gentle. You squint up at the blue sky and pretend you have no body, that you are floating. Your eyes close. You drift.

In the seconds between sleep and waking, a door swings open. You see:

Your father sitting next to your mother by her bed.

It's familiar, this fragment, you have seen it before.

The woodpigeon in the yew tree chortles to itself, throat swelling.

———

The knife slices through the fleshy roots beautifully, efficiently. It is an elegant knife with an oiled wooden handle and brass trim, a stainless steel blade that unfolds out of the handle and locks open. The woman in the shop showed you how to use it; you have to press the metal spine to 'break' the blade and fold it back into its handle. She did this smoothly, smiling into your eyes as she did it, as if the two of you were conspiring.

The knife is very sharp. You use a whetstone to keep it that way, sharpening it at least once a week, rubbing the blade in single slow strokes at an angle.

Mr Holub loves the bearded irises, their lobed flowers and purple velvet tongues. You think the tongues are sloppy, prefer the tightly wrapped, pointed packages of the buds before they open. And you like the leaves, fresh clean sabres of bluegreen.

The horizontal roots live half in, half out of the sandy soil. You are digging them up and dividing them, creating new plants now the old ones have finished flowering. You cut healthy chunks of root with leaves attached, then trim the leaves, cutting across them sharply, making a short fan shape like Mr Holub once showed you with a deft slice of his own sharp knife.

'Cut them so,' he said, 'Like this. Then they keep more water while new roots come.'

You miss the old man; he spends so little time here now. Martin says his joints give him too much trouble, especially his hands; he wouldn't be able to use the knife safely. You wonder if he is still rolling his own cigarettes.

You replant the irises just beneath the soil in plastic pots and water them in. The air is full of the scent of damp soil, roses and sweet peas. The papery blue nigella is flowering too. You can't see it without thinking about planting the seeds with Matti early in the spring. You hope he visits again while it's still flowering so you can show him what Love-in-a-Mist looks like. Perhaps you will ask Martin to invite him this weekend.

You think about Matti's small body, his head bent over the seed trays, the soft nape of his neck. Matti trusts that the world is a good place. He has no reason to believe differently, not yet. His parents are happy. Martin is a playful, affectionate uncle. And Matti has Mr Holub for his grandfather. You see:

> *The little boy and the old man, walking down the path together, surveying the plants. The old man is nodding as he listens to the little boy's stream of chatter. He points out a new bud and the little boy darts forward, has to touch it. The old man smiles and tells him, 'Careful, it is not a strong one that. Not strong like a boy!' And the two of them laugh.*

You recognise the feeling that thickens in you: envy. But your affection for Matti makes it possible for you to be glad for him. You line up the pots of new iris plants in the sun.

———

Later, at the windmill.

'You're always saying how much you learn from her,' says Martin. 'How much she shows you about yourself. Have you ever wondered what she gets out of it? Or is it just a big ego trip for her?'

You feel a flutter of annoyance in the centre of your chest and wait long enough to let it settle before speaking.

'No,' you say, with absolute calm. It's not a one-way thing. I get a lot out of the time I spend with Evie. But she gets something out of it too. She's telling me about her life. Things she has never told anyone before.'

You watch an ant climbing up your boot, brush it off before it disappears into your sock.

'She takes risks,' you say, 'She tells me about things that make her vulnerable. She trusts me not to judge her.'

Martin sits cross-legged with his back against the curved wall of the windmill. He doesn't comment, just glances your way and then turns his attention back to his pear. He bites off the stem and spits it out, then takes another bite and chews slowly.

'And if you think about it,' you continue, more to yourself than to him, 'She must appreciate having someone else to spend time with. Someone other than Margaret Keyes, I mean.'

Evie looks forward to my visits.

I bring something valuable to her life.

You breathe in, feel your chest expand. Like something blossoming.

Last time, you had arrived to find Evie out of bed, sitting in the brown brocade chair. It was shocking to see her like that, propped upright with the cushions, awkward, her chin resting on her chest. But when she spoke, she lifted her head to look at you.

'Margaret Keyes has decided I need a change,' she said. 'I didn't make it easy for her, though.' Her lovely eyes glinted. 'I have perfected the art of becoming a dead weight.'

'You've been teasing her again,' you said, trying not to smile. How strange it was to see Evie upright, even this floppy upright that depended so entirely on the chair to support her. You sat at the headboard end of the bed, Evie's end, and thought: this is how she sees the world. From here, there's the window, the mantelpiece, the chair. It's an entirely different angle on the room. From your usual end at the foot of the bed, you see Evie and little else.

'Don't you like having a change?' you asked.

Evie sighed. 'I do. But more so when it is at my own instigation.'

You saw:

> *Margaret peeling back Evie's bedclothes, exposing the still, pale legs, scooping her up under the arms, grunting as she heaved the unresponsive body into the chair. After stripping the bedclothes and making the bed, she ignored Evie's demands to be put back.*
>
> *'You need a change,' said Margaret, leaving her there, in the chair, uncomfortable and unable to reach her radio.*

Martin has finished the pear. He throws the core into the bushes at the edge of the clearing.

'Last time I went,' you say, 'Evie was sitting up. In the chair next to her bed.'

'Does that mean she's getting better?' asks Martin.

'I don't think so.'

But imagine if it did.

Imagine if your connection with her was making a difference – helping to heal her mind and body.

The thought unfolds sweetly in your mind.

'Better go back in five minutes,' says Martin. He slides further down against the windmill until he is lying flat in the grass. Where his shirt rides up, his stomach is flat and solid. He pats out a drumbeat on his own ribcage.

———

14

Margaret opens the door. You don't want to look at the grey moon of her face, you wait for her to move aside so you can get past her to Evie.

'She's not here,' says Margaret.

'What?'

She can't not be here.

'She has to go to the hospital sometimes, for tests. It's routine. She told me to call and tell you but I didn't,' Margaret's voice is higher pitched than usual. She looks just over your head as she speaks.

'I wanted you to come. I wanted to talk to you.'

She is breathing hard, as though she has run from somewhere and just arrived; her face is gleaming.

'Will you stay and have a cup of tea?' she asks in that strange strained voice.

You nod. And then you stand there, both of you in the doorway, uncertain, like dancers who have forgotten the steps. Finally, Margaret lunges to the left and backs into the house. You follow her through the second door on the left *oh god, this is Evie's house, Evie used to walk through this doorway* into a light room with a high ceiling, with moulded cornices and coving, a grey marble fireplace, a vibrant green rug on the floor in front of it. There's an ironing board, a laundry basket, and a heavy round table covered in freshly ironed, neatly folded clothes. You recognise Evie's plum silk tunic. And there's a pile of grey flannel that must belong to Margaret.

She leads you through this room, through another door, into the kitchen. There is a white porcelain sink with a wooden draining board, but there are no kitchen units. Instead, pieces of furniture that have been adapted – beautiful chests of drawers, bookcases, a wardrobe. Some are fitted under shiny work surfaces; some stand alone; all are painted in peacock colours so that somehow they belong together, completely right for Evie. She must have designed this before she got ill, you think. It's perfect for her. And so wrong for Margaret Keyes.

> Grey limpet, Margaret, completely out of place on this bright reef.

The kitchen table is huge. You imagine Evie holding court here, late at night, sharing caviar and crackers with her friends after a night at the theatre. Drinking black coffee with whisky or rum. Moving, later, to another room; somewhere with soft cushions, a chaise longue.

The table has green legs, a polished wooden top that undulates gently. You pull up a chair, a plain chair with a tasselled tapestry cushion. You sit with your palms flat in front of you on the tabletop, enjoying the coolness of the wood. Margaret Keyes makes tea; she boils the water in a metal kettle on the range.

'She'd buy me an electric one if I wanted. I prefer this.'

You don't respond. But you look up, consider Margaret's back, her buttocks encased in pale pink jogpants, then look away.

The kitchen is on the ground floor. The wide window above the sink is partially overgrown with ivy. The incoming light is filtered through chlorophyll, tinted green. It slides in over the windowsill, enters the room slowly.

You stroke the grain of the tabletop with the ball of your thumb and check your guts for anxiety. There is none, just a faint buzzing within the warm loops that could be excitement.

Margaret Keyes brings the brown teapot. The milk is still in the bottle, the sugar still in its packet, as if you shouldn't settle in. Then she sits, not opposite you, but at a right angle, so you are on one long side, facing the window, and she is at the head of the table. You hear her chair creak, feel the table brace itself as she rests her elbows on it. There's the quiet pouring of the tea. She gives you your usual mug, reaches for the milk.

'Actually, Margaret, if you don't mind, I'd prefer a bit less milk in mine.'

The bright brown eyes in that soft pastry face harden for a moment; she didn't like that. And just in case you were in any doubt, she makes a point of putting in the tiniest amount of milk. Half a teaspoonful.

'That enough?"

'A bit more, thanks.'

So she adds more milk, a lot more, with an I told you so look on her face. But her hand shakes as she picks up her own mug and she puts it down again without drinking. She notices you noticing and folds both her hands on the hams of her lap. She sucks in her bottom lip. Her eyes are damp.

Oh no, don't cry, Margaret.

I can't comfort you. I don't like you.

'Do you spend much time in the garden?' you ask, speaking into the space in front of you, giving her a chance to make her face behave. She clears her throat and words lurch out of her.

'No. Not much. I don't like it out there. It's creepy.'

'I've seen it from upstairs,' you say, your eyes still aimed at the window. 'It looks like it hasn't been touched for a while. But there are some good shrubs amongst all that tangle. It could be nice again.'

In your peripheral vision you see her raise her hands. She wipes her palms over the thick curve of her brows and cheeks, smoothing the upset away. Now she sips her tea, both hands wrapped around the mug. And now she seems to remember that this is, to all intents and purposes, her kitchen, her territory. She breathe in, lifts her shoulders. A tap starts to drip in the background.

Prip.

'It would be nice to have a garden I could use,' she says. 'My flat is downstairs, in the basement. It's quite dark, what with all the ivy and bushes.'

You imagine a cavern, its mouth hidden behind a tangle of roots and whippy branches. Somewhere a troll might live, a troll in a pink jogsuit. Now you have to say something or you'll smirk.

'How long have you been here, Margaret?'

'A few years. She wasn't so ill when I first came. It's only this last year she's taken completely to her bed.'

Prip.

Margaret scratches at the cuff of her sleeve, produces a crumpled tissue, blows her nose, making a very dry sound of it. You recognise displacement activity when you see it. But you hate blowing your nose in front of anyone. Funny she finds it reassuring.

'I did a course,' says Margaret suddenly. 'You know. How to lift people. Avoiding bedsores. What to do in an emergency.' Her eyes settle on the rim of her mug. 'I'd never done this kind of work before. I thought – how hard could it be? Just one small woman. And she seemed nice.'

You remember the spats you've witnessed between Evie and Margaret. You know how Evie feels about her. You see:

> *Evie's face, almost ugly with the strength of her feeling after Margaret leaves the room.*
>
> *'Intolerable woman. And the worst of it, Claire, dear, is that she has so little self-respect. Wouldn't you leave, if you knew you were so very much disliked by your employer?'*

102

'But why does she stay?"

'As I say, dear, she has no self-respect. She is weak willed. Or perhaps she thinks she will inherit my money when I die.' Laughter like cold water over gravel.

'Why *do* you stay, Margaret? Have you never thought about leaving, about working somewhere where you could feel happier and more appreciated?'

She sighs. The sound of a grey pillowcase billowing in the wind.

'I have to stay.'

'Is it the – I mean, do you feel you've invested a lot here and you need to see it through?'

Her eyes narrow.

You persevere. 'Has Evie any family? Any relations or friends?'

> You know what I'm getting at, don't you, Margaret? Are you going to make a big show of being offended? As though Evie's inheritance has never crossed your mind?

'You think it's about her money,' she states flatly.

'Well I wouldn't necessarily blame you if it was...'

Prip.

'You've been coming here for quite a while now,' she says.

'Yes.'

You're pretty sure Margaret could tell you exactly how many weeks it is since you first rang the doorbell.

'Do you have any idea how much longer you'll be coming?'

'As long as I'm welcome,' you say. 'Evie has asked me to continue.' You pause, savouring the triumph of the moment. 'And to consider coming twice a week in future.'

Ha.

Margaret's face is strangely unreadable.

'You'll agree?' she asks.

'I don't see why not. I know you and she have a difficult

relationship. At least, that's what I gather from the way you are when you're in the same room together. But I like her, Margaret. I probably get to see a side of her that you don't know about.'

Special me.

Margaret snorts.

What is that?

Is that sow noise a laugh?

'I've seen lots of different sides of Evie,' she says. 'I'd be surprised if I haven't seen the one she shows you.' Her face is flushed red. With amusement? Anger? You remember that this woman has the most intimate of relationships with Evie. Feeds her. Washes her. Assists her in every way.

Don't beat around the bush. She puts a pot under Evie's backside several times a day so she can take a pee or a crap. She wipes her afterwards. Wouldn't she know Evie better than anyone?

No, it doesn't work like that. That's enforced physical intimacy – the only way to survive it is to put up barriers, wear a mask.

Evie once said – *'When you depend on another person for your most basic needs, they have enormous power over you.'* You remember the times she has hinted that Margaret is unkind.

'Do you often lose your patience with her, Margaret? It must be easy to take it out on her – be just a bit rough with flannel? Perhaps not hear the bell when she needs something to drink?'

Margaret scowls.

'No easier than it is for her to take it out on me. Leave it too late for me to get the bedpan, so the sheets need changing. Wait until she knows I'm sitting down to watch the telly before ringing for something small, something we both know she doesn't need. And she has the last word about things, of course. I wanted to keep a cat in my room. She wouldn't budge on that. It would have been company for me.'

She seems to notice how loud she's speaking. Stops. Sniffs.

Prip.

You sip your tea. Lukewarm.

'So why *don't* you leave, Margaret?'

'I can't leave,' she says. 'Because of my son.'

She scowls again. Seems annoyed to have to explain.

'He was born with problems,' she goes on. 'Disabilities. He's a grown man now, but he needs special care.'

Now she isn't annoyed, just matter of fact. 'I couldn't afford it on my own, you see. Not the kind of place that would really care. Evie pays for my son to be looked after. Somewhere good and safe, where the staff can be trusted to treat him well.'

You didn't know this. Evie has never mentioned this.

Why hasn't Evie mentioned this?

Prip.

Margaret gets up and lumbers over to the sink. Tightens the tap into silence.

'Can I use the loo before I go?' you ask.

———

The toilet is on the first floor, opposite Evie's room. It's disappointing, could be any toilet in any house. When you're finished, instead of going straight back downstairs, you peek round Evie's door, knowing she's not there, wanting to see what her room is like when she's not in it.

The empty bed is shocking. A flash of white sheet shows from under the velvet and chenille of her bedspread and cushions. You look away, focus on the glut of rich fabrics spilling out of the wardrobe and the sheen of expensive things, breathe the dry spicy scent that has become so familiar. On the surface, the room is the same, but the clock rustles through the seconds. If Evie were here, the gaps between them would seem longer.

The room next door is a small storeroom. There are shelves, folded sheets and towels. A bedpan. Other stuff related to Evie's medical needs. There is a glass case, like a large bathroom cabinet, full of brown bottles and small round plastic tubs. Medicines. You wonder what she takes.

You consider the other doors on this landing and weigh up your choices, decide to investigate them later, if there's time. You want to see upstairs. You want to be at the top of the house.

The wooden banister is warm under your hand. Your palm tingles. The stairs groan under you, in pleasure, as if they have missed the weight of feet. The carpet is like a sponge; your steps sound like shallow breathing. You climb steadily. At each landing, there's a window that lets in the sun and gives you a slightly higher perspective on the garden below. Then, three floors up, the carpet gives way to bare floorboards and a layer of dust that rises above your shoes and dances around your knees. The motes sparkle like house sprites, leading you up the stairs, their light voices calling ahead.

'*She's coming! She's coming!*'

Two more flights, the stairs become narrower, the banisters less ornate.

'*She's coming!*'

Breathless, you reach the top landing, and then there's nowhere else to go, just one door, a small white wooden door, and you open it and you're there, in the highest room in the house.

'*She's here!*'

The sprites announce you, chattering, then settle. You stand in the middle of the room, pulse beating in your temples and wrists.

It's dry and light in here. Too bright for a room with such a small window. There are ripples in the air, reflections in the corners. You have to close your eyes as you stand in the centre of the small room catching your breath, the sound of blood rushing in your ears. You wait for the pulsing of your body to slow. And it does. Your blood and your breathing become calm. You are calm. The air is soft, a presence around you. It holds you, strokes you. And your body responds.

It's the house, you realize. The house wants you here.

'I could be yours.'

Sitting now, back flat against a warm wall, palms flat on the bare boards, you breathe in the light and the air. It fills your lungs, your stomach, settles in the cradle of your pelvis. You keep your eyelids shut, sink into the sensations.

'I could be yours.'

The floor cushions you. The wall supports you. You could stay here forever.

'Yours. When she's gone. One day.'

No.

This isn't right.

You open your eyes.

The sunlight has faded; the room is full of shadows. The floor is hard underneath you. You stand up, brush off the dust, and leave quickly, shutting the white door behind you without looking back.

Margaret is waiting for you at the bottom of the stairs, wants to say more before you go.

'Things aren't always what they seem, you know. She lies there so still, looking so small.'

'What are you saying, Margaret? That she's not as sick as she looks? That she's pretending?'

'Just that you should look more closely, maybe. That she might not be everything you think she is. That's all.'

She follows you to the door; casts nervous words after you as you step outside.

'It would be better if you didn't tell her about today. About coming to see me.'

'I didn't come to see you.'

Margaret's eyes are desperate. 'I know. I mean – '

'It's okay,' you tell her. 'I won't say a word.'

———

15

'**Y**ou know, Claire, I would have given a lot to have been as tall as you are.'

You draw yourself in.

'No,' she says, 'Don't do that. Don't protect yourself against me. I know – I absolutely know – that people have hurt you with their clumsy reassurances about your height. That isn't what I'm doing, my dear, I promise you.'

She holds you with her eyes, and it's as if she could reach out physically.

'This is the truth, Claire. When you are older, when you look back at yourself as you are now, it will make your heart ache that you didn't know how lovely you were.'

You want to shrug, laugh, make light of this. But Evie is too serious.

'You'll look back and you'll wish someone had told you, made you believe it. You'll wish you could reach back and tell your younger self to be proud of your body, to enjoy it.'

Is that all it takes to feel beautiful?

The ability to stand ahead of yourself in time and look back?

'Make sure you have lots of photographs of yourself, my dear. And when you look at them, try to imagine what you'll feel as an old woman looking back at your younger self. Let it be a gift from the old woman you'll become.'

Evie means it. And her stillness seems to underline what she is saying; it gives her words emphasis.

The paralysed woman never lies. Is that it?

In your throat there's a sound like a latch unclicking. You cough.

On the way back to the station, you stop at a pharmacy. You need tissues. You need toothpaste. At the checkout, you smile at the girl behind the counter, study the perfect stroke of her black eyeliner as she looks down at the till, ringing up your purchases. And at the last minute, you pick up a disposable camera.

'I'll take this too.'

—

16

Evie says:

'From the age of twelve or thirteen, I began to re-invent myself. I wanted to look different. I insisted that everything bought for me was plain, no patterns – just plain clothes in good colours. When I was young, my hair was dark, you know. Darker than yours. I looked good in blues and greens. I had a kind of style even then.'

Even though she is speaking with her eyes closed, you can see the satisfaction in her face.

'In summer, after school, I started taking long walks along the seafront. From one side of town – my family's side of town – to the other, where a different kind of people lived. Where I live now, Claire. I used to walk up the wide avenues and the crescents, peering in to people's homes if the curtains were open. Some rooms had chandeliers. I loved the people who lived in those homes.

'I loved the women whose fingernails were always perfect, who had the glowing skin that only expensive make-up achieves. I loved them for their beautifully cut clothes, for the fact that they could choose what they wanted without looking at the price. Their clothes had elegant shapes and finely crafted details, fabric that hung perfectly around their bodies. I loved the fact that everything in their lives smelled good; they carried the cumulative scent of expensive things with them. Silk linings and perfectly turned seams. Shoes that fitted, soft leather that supported their feet.

'I loved the men for their confidence. Even the ugly men; they were sure of themselves. Some were loud, some quiet. But they all seemed to have a sense of assurance, the knowledge that there was little beyond their reach.'

She sighs.

'Of course, one day I would realize that these people were just as unhappy, just as unable to satisfy themselves, as the people from my own background. And I would despise them for that. But for now, I was captivated. I would walk slowly past the entrances to the grand hotels, trying to see inside. A doorman asked me once if I was looking for someone. And I used my new voice to answer him. After that, I would speak to as many people as I could. I was always on the lookout for someone to engage with; I manufactured opportunities by asking directions, or just saying, 'Good afternoon. Isn't it a lovely day?'

'In bed at night I would replay these small conversations, extending them, creating imagined outcomes. The man in the silver car turned out to be my real father, whisked me off to a whole new life. The woman coming out of an expensive shop was charmed by my witty conversation and wanted a travelling companion, took me around the world with her.

'One man did ask if I wanted to go for a drink and I said no. I regretted it later. I wished I had gone with him, even though I knew what he wanted. I had little sexual experience at that time, but I was still keenly aware of the forces of desire and pleasure, I knew how much they could motivate. In the long run, however, it turned out to be the better decision. Things worked out extremely well.

'I was determined to create my own rags to riches story, you see. I didn't know then that transformation runs deeper than wealth and manners. I didn't know and I didn't care. I just wanted to be rich. And that's why, in the end, I married Harold Bell.'

She opens her eyes and smiles at you. You wait until you are sure she is not going to continue. Then you ask:

'Were you never frightened, Evie, when you walked in strange places on your own? Never scared that someone might hurt you?'

You imagine yourself, out alone at that age. You would have been anxious.

'You know, my dear, strangely, I never was frightened. I think the glamour I associated with the people I was watching must have convinced me I was safe amongst them, amongst their houses.'

She tilts her head, remembering.

'The funny thing, Claire, is that I never went walking again, not after I met Harold. I spent all those hours walking, hundreds of hours, I should imagine. And as soon as I got what I wanted, I stopped. Just like that.'

'You didn't actually enjoy it then?

'Not walking for its own sake, no. Although,' she smiles, 'I do miss it now. Sometimes I lie here and try to remember what it felt like, to put one foot in front of the other. To feel the ground pressing up against my feet.'

You look away for a moment, then back at her face.

'I read something, at the library,' you say, carefully. 'A theory – that paralysis could be caused if someone turned their emotional difficulties into physical symptoms...' you trail off.

Evie narrows her eyes.

'My dear, did you know that, until relatively recently, it was thought that hysterical symptoms like paralysis originated in the uterus? And the Ancient Greeks believed that the womb moved around the body, causing symptoms wherever it settled.'

She smiles, but without humour.

'Theories come and go, don't they?' she says.

—

Packed tight in your hand, the stack of hazel leaves is like a deck of cards, pliable and solid. But when you place them on the ground, individually, each leaf overlapping, they are like the feathers of a bird. Or the scales of a fish. You tuck them up against the trunk of a young beech tree, lapping against its roots. You place them alternately topside up, underside up, creating the effect of light on water. You work round the tree, radiating out.

When you stand up and step back to look, the tree is rising out of a shining green pool.

———

17

'You can't go straight up today,' says Margaret Keyes. 'She has someone with her.'

So you wait in the hallway, stiff on one of the straight-backed chairs. Margaret has gone back to the kitchen. You close your eyes and breathe in the scent of beeswax. The air around you is agitated, pricks the skin on your forearms. The house is tense. The house disapproves.

> Whoever's here is not welcome, is that it? Someone you don't want?

Above you, you feel – or you imagine it – the vibration of a masculine voice.

Rumble. Silence. Rumble. Silence.

Then quiet for a long time.

You wonder where he's sitting, this man in Evie's room. At the end of her bed where you sit?

> Surely not.

You recognise the feeling that wraps itself around your shoulders, light, scratchy, a cape of metal feathers. Jealousy.

> Is this how Margaret felt when I came?
> Did she sit down here, straining to hear, hating me for intruding?

Abruptly, the door upstairs is opened, the sudden increase in volume makes you jump.

' – get back to you within the next few days. Always a pleasure to see you, Mrs Bell. Good bye.'

You watch him appear down the stairs: soft black shoes, dark trouser legs, a black brief case held stiffly in a pale plump hand. Lilac shirt, blue tie, dark jacket, mottled throat. Finally, a pink face, as though he has rubbed it too hard, or sat in the sun for too long. And wispy fair hair.

As he reaches the bottom of the stairs, Margaret Keyes appears out of nowhere, lets him out. Then she turns around, resting her back against the door as though she's tired.

'Her solicitor,' she says, without expression, raising her eyebrows at you. You raise yours back. The idea flaps between you, huge and clumsy and insistent, like a giant fledgling, but neither of you speaks out loud.

She's only gone and changed her will, hasn't she?

What else could it be?

Margaret thumps heavy-heeled back to the kitchen. You go on up.

—

Evie's photo album is covered in soft black leather, the corners are capped in silver. You hold it on your lap, turning the pages slowly, hearing the crackle as they respond after years closed tight shut.

There is a wedding photograph: a group of people on the steps of a church. Evie stands out of course, the girl with dark hair and no veil, intense and vivid. Her plain white dress is high at the neck and long sleeved, exquisitely fitted, her bouquet a burst of white flowers. She is staring directly down the lens, triumphant.

The man standing next to her must be Harold. He has eyes

only for Evie, is not even aware that the photograph has been taken. His profile reveals the softness of his chin.

There are other people, looking formal, stiff. Two older men and a woman.

'Who are these people?'

'Harold's brothers and sister. He was the youngest of five children, an afterthought or an accident.'

'You didn't invite any of your own family?'

'Of course not.'

Another photograph: Evie is leaning against a low wall. Behind her, the sea is impossibly blue, the extraordinary blue of postcards. But it is Evie that stands out. Her dark hair is short and sleek, her light brown eyes full of intelligence. The angles of her face are beautiful. She leans back with absolute confidence, her hands resting lightly on the top of the wall, and the wind moulds the turquoise cotton of her blouse against the planes of her body.

Another: Evie at the centre of a group of people dressed in evening wear. She wears a sheath of violet, glimmering. The other women in the picture seem pale and fussy by comparison.

'Is Grace Cullen in this one?' you ask, wondering if she will notice that you have remembered her best friend's name.

Evie frowns. 'No,' she says. 'Grace would never permit anyone to take her photograph.'

—

The shop is warm and quiet. The thin dust stirs and sticks to you as you move among the shelves. You tidy green plastic bottles of plant food, yellow sachets of weed killer. You make sure the rows are straight, with no obvious gaps. Then you sit behind the counter, rest your arms on the dark wood, rest your head on your arms, and breathe gently, trying to ignore the smell of peat and plant food.

Glamour. You were fairly sure you knew what it meant,

but you had checked in the dictionary anyway. It isn't just about beauty and sophistication. It means magic. Enchantment.

When Evie had first discovered the world of wealthy people, everything about it seemed glamorous to her. Looking for an escape from the life she loathed, she hadn't been seeing clearly. Her eyes had been full of her own dreams.

Now, though, Evie knows better. She sees things as they are. She sees you, faults and all, and still wants to spend time with you.

You raise your head, prop your chin on your forearm, scan the gloomy shop as if you have never seen it before. The bottles and boxes squat in their rows, bright colours glowing.

It's good to value things as they are. The ordinary things you already have.

A breeze from the open doorway cools one side of your face.

Next to *glamour*, there had been *glance*. To glide off an object instead of striking it fully. To look at something briefly.

You don't know what to do with your mouth. It feels tense, uncomfortable. You can imagine how awkward you must look through the lens.

'Right. Smile now,' says Martin from behind the disposable camera, and you reveal your teeth. He takes the photograph.

'Thanks Martin, that's fine,' you say, moving towards him, hand outstretched to take the camera.

'No, you need another one just in case that doesn't come out,' he steps away from you, holding the camera above his head so you can't reach it.

'Alright, one more. Quickly. I hate this.'

This time you smile tight-lipped. No teeth. Martin takes another photograph and hands the camera back.

'Hope they come out alright,' he says.

'They'll be fine. He only asked for a snapshot.'

You have lied to Martin, told him that the photo is for your father; that he asked for it.

'If you would sit still longer, we could get some really nice ones. We could go over by the roses or against the fence and get a nicer background.'

'No,' you say again. 'This is fine.'

———

Dearest Claire,

The days pass quickly now. I wake up one morning, sunlight. Doze, wake up again, it's night.

I want to hold on to the hours, but I'm very tired now. Can't remember if I saw you today or was it yesterday I'm not sure. Your father seems always to be here when I wake. I asked him where you were. He said school. I had forgotten for a moment that some things haven't changed.

When I am gone Claire, he will need you. You must look after him. It's not fair to ask you. None of this is fair. Make sure he is alright please.

All my love.

You refold the page, press it back into the envelope, toss it towards the wooden box on the writing bureau. Even now, your mother has the power to astonish you. That she could leave you so carelessly and still expect you to look after your father – surprise still flickers alongside anger.

Oh god. Will this ever stop mattering?

The duck egg room glows around you. Lying flat on the new cream carpet, you bend your knees and adjust the distance between your feet until you find the spot where gravity keeps your legs in the most comfortable position. You shut your eyes. You see:

Yourself, seven or eight, in the garden in autumn. You

have been collecting yellow leaves to press between the pages of a book. You look up to find your mother standing at the window watching, and you wave. But she does not wave back. Your arm stops, drops.

Your mother is not watching you. Your father is due home. She is watching the front gate.

You can still feel the secret small embarrassment of that; it's the same private deflation that happens even now, as an adult, when a smile is not returned. You open your eyes.

Your mother had no close friends in the village, although she was a social creature. People often visited, shared coffee with her. Strong coffee in small cups. Once, you were working in your little square of garden as your mother showed a visitor out. She stopped to point out your tidy rows of plants. You knelt in the earth, looking up at their nodding faces as your mother explained.

'Claire is so neat and tidy. She loves this little garden. She can tidy the poor plants to her heart's content.' She smiled her fondness at you and then shifted her focus to include the visitor in this moment of intimacy.

'It isn't that, Mum,' you said. 'I just like to see them grow. They all start off as a seed, and they turn into a plant that has hundreds of seeds of its own. Don't you think that's amazing?'

'She has always been tidy,' your mother continued. 'As a little girl she put her teddies and dolls in rows.' Affectionate laughter. She moved away and the visitor followed her, an obedient satellite.

'I myself have never been that tidy,' you heard your mother saying, as they moved off down the path. 'I prefer a more natural garden, a place where there is total freedom to grow.' She made nature sound like her own creation, one she could take credit for.

The floor is solid under your back. The duck egg walls are sympathetic.

When Evie listens, you feel sure that you are seen and heard. Sometimes when you are talking, Evie says nothing at all, but her eyes never leave your face. And sometimes, she listens so hard she even hears the words you have not spoken.

—

On the way out of the house, you pick up the disposable camera. Today, instead of gathering things, you are going to take photographs of them. There are thirty-six exposures on the film and Martin only took two photographs of you; you have plenty to play around with. You walk slowly, looking at the world through sharp eyes, seeking out the details.

A clump of moss. Lush, tiny starbursts of green. It is damp and abundant to the eye, like a miniature tropical forest, but strangely dry to the touch. You take fourteen photographs of the moss, from different angles, some closer, some further away. But the disposable camera does not offer any focusing options, you can only point and click. Through the viewfinder, the moss looks a long way away.

You take thirteen shots of a silver birch, trying to catch the sheen of its papery trunk, the patterns in the flaking bark, the secret shine of newly revealed layers. You try looking down the trunk. Then you lie on your back, looking up; the light catches the ripples in the wood.

In the churchyard, you take seven photographs of the lichen on James Frank Strong's headstone. You are amazed at the flatness of it. Even when you run your finger over the patches of lichen, you can't feel anything but the texture of the stone. The lichen is inert, in colours of old chewing gum and rust. You do not even know if it is alive.

When you have used up all the film, you sit against the gravestone with your eyes half closed, eyelashes creating a fringed edge on the world. The sun is warm on your bare arms. The wind is as loud as the sea, buffeting the trees, flipping their leaves over to reveal silver undersides. The sound is unsettling but you are sheltered here. The sun soaks into your skin. The warmth is soothing. You close your eyes completely and concentrate only on feeling the sun, hearing the wind.

The wind blows through you; you are nothing but warmth.

—

Home again later, unlocking the front door, the shiny new addition to your keyring is still a surprise; it stands out amongst the familiar shapes and weights of the other keys. When Evie gave it to you, she had spoken lightly and laughed. But something good had unfolded in your chest, something important.

'Look,' she had said, soon after you arrived. 'There is something for you on the mantelpiece.' It was a white envelope, propped up against a blue glass candleholder. When you picked it up, you felt the metal shape through the paper. You unsealed the envelope, tipped the key into your waiting palm and it shone there.

'It makes sense, dear. There's no need for Margaret to come running to open the door every time you arrive. Now you can just let yourself in.'

You looked at the key for what seemed like a long time, not knowing what to say, your eyes stinging.

'Don't be a goose, Claire, it's just a key.' Evie had laughed, but with real affection.

'Thanks,' you said, laughing too. And you put it in your pocket.

Later, when you added it to your keyring, you stroked the new brass teeth of it and thought 'Margaret must have had to organise this. She must have waited for it to be cut, put it in the envelope. She must have sealed the envelope with her own mouth.'

That would have given her something to be grumpy about.

But for once there was little sense of triumph. You found yourself feeling sorry for Margaret, who has so obviously lost whatever battle she was trying to win against you. Evie has made it clear: she has created a special place for you in her life.

She has given me the key to her house.

She has changed her Will.

Standing in the hall, fingers closed loosely around the weight of keys in your hand, you shake your head, as if to dislodge the thought. You put the keys down on the table, where they settle into a chunk of angles, next to the disposable camera.

—

18

In the seconds between sleep and waking, there is nothing. Nothing dragging behind you, nothing to defend against. Just a quiet lifting out of sleep and the gentle morning sun glowing through the curtains.

———

Evie says:

'Do you remember losing your virginity, Claire?'

The question hangs in the air; Evie's eyes are shut; you know better than to offer an answer. She continues:

'I was sixteen when I had my first experience of sexual intercourse. Gerald Hurley was older than me, about eighteen, I think. He seemed very much older to me then, of course, very grown up. He worked at the local cinema, wore a red jacket that was too small for him, he sat at the window and sold the tickets. He used to let his friends in for free.

'Gerald and I had been courting for a few weeks. At that stage we had done little more than holding hands, kissing, that endless exploratory kissing that teenagers do. He had stroked my breasts, pressed himself against me. I loved the sensation, the buzzing warmth that took over my whole body. And I felt such a sense of power, knowing I could call it up in him, that desire. He was hoarse with it, wretched with it.

'One night, I stayed behind after the late film. I hid in the back row when the lights came on, waited for him in the dark after they were switched off for the night. I waited among the velvet seats, full of excitement. I expected this to be even more fun, more passionate. When he arrived and sat next to me, we talked about the film. Then he took off his jacket and we lay down on the top step in the aisle. The carpet was very thin. He was quick. It hurt. And when it was over, still lying on top of me, he asked 'So how many times have you done that?' and I said 'Never before,' and he laughed as he rolled off and said it had been too easy.

'I have never forgotten it. The carpet scratchy and the step hard under me. I was sore and wet from his ejaculation. And furious; it was a kind of rage I had never experienced before. I decided then that I would never again allow a man to make me feel ashamed. That I would never give myself away again. And I never did, you know. I married Harold. But I didn't give myself to him, ever.'

Evie pauses, waits for her breathing to calm.

'Anyway, as it turns out, my dear, I soon had other things to deal with. Cross as he may have been, Gerald was a highly potent young man. I missed my next menstrual period, and the one after that. I was pregnant.

'Of course, this happens all the time nowadays. But I was sixteen, remember, and this was a long time ago, before such things became commonplace. My mother was as ashamed as she had ever been in her life; her shame made her spiteful. My father drew away from me, at last. The children in the neighbourhood were cruel, of course, as children are.

'And I was oblivious to it all. For the first four or five months, I was so completely thrilled with the experience of pregnancy that nothing else mattered. There was an extraordinary sense of companionship in it – a spark of someone else always with me. This was the level of closeness I had always craved.

'Even my beloved little brother was excluded. With this extraordinary thing happening, I didn't need him. I neglected him. He was hurt, angry. The intense love he had always felt for me flipped into something very close to hatred. I'm sure it would have broken my heart – if I had been able to feel anything beyond what was happening in my own body. But in those first few months, I needed no-one. I had become a whole world within myself.'

Evie is silent. You wonder if she has finished speaking. She takes a deep breath and continues:

'A bit further on, as the baby grew inside me, things changed. It was so much more than I was prepared for – it demanded such a great deal of room. And I was trapped, there was nothing I could do but carry it. On more than a few occasions, I was literally on the edge of panic. I didn't see how both of us could survive the whole nine months together.

'And then she was born. I didn't think I would survive that, either. But after eleven hours, she slid into the world and was wrapped up, taken away. I never held her. It was the strangest feeling, afterwards, pressing my breasts, watching warm milk run down my body.

'I was left empty. And my brother, by then, was hard and unforgiving; it was not an easy time. But I got over it. One has to get over these things, you see. Either do something about them, or get over them.'

Evie opens her eyes. Looks straight at you with something akin to ferocity.

'But that child will always be mine,' she says. 'She belongs to me and she will be mine until the day she dies.'

You nod, but she has already settled back again, eyes closed.

'It wasn't long after that, a few months perhaps, that my mother left, taking my brother with her. I came back to the house one evening to find my father in the kitchen, smoking, his face wet with tears. She hadn't even left a note, just taken what they needed, left her wedding ring on the table.

'I started walking more than ever. I became addicted to it, desperate to leave my circumstances and my thoughts behind me. I didn't know it then, my dear, but in less time than I could have imagined, my life would change beyond all recognition.'

She pauses and you risk a question.

'Did you miss your mother after she was gone?' There is tension in your throat; it is important to know this.

'I'm not certain I did.' She hesitates, blinks. 'I think the truth is that I hated her for leaving us. It was a betrayal. She had no right to just remove herself without warning. She should have changed things, somehow. Made demands. That passive withdrawal could not be answered. It could not be dealt with.'

Evie shakes her head slowly, as though it is heavy.

'That's enough about that for now, Claire.'

—

You paid extra to have the photographs developed within the hour. You hadn't intended to do that. There was no hurry – it had taken you a week to remember to take them into the shop. But you discovered, when the man behind the counter asked you, that you wanted them as soon as possible.

Now you have a glossy yellow envelope. You push the car seat right back, give yourself legroom. The car smells of warm upholstery and of the bunch of sunflowers on the back seat. They are small redbrown sunflowers, not the huge yellow plates *seeds like perfect capsules, heart-shaped kernels, silvergreybeige nutty sweet flavour* you used to grow as a child. The smell of sunflowers is not sweet; it is dry and dusty, as though the petals are hoarding their moisture and won't spare any for scent.

You take out the sheaf of photographs, enjoying the significant weight of them, the stiffness of the shiny bundle.

But the photographs themselves are disappointing. The moss that had been so fascinating and so intricate: a dull green sponge. The luminous silver birch bark: simply pale. The lichen on the gravestones: a blur.

You flick through the whole pile quickly, searching for anything that resembles what you saw when you took it. And then all at once there are the photographs Martin took of you. You had forgotten them. You are unprepared. For an instant, you see yourself as others might see you: a young woman, very young, with a narrow face and dark eyes. She is uncertain, her head awkward, her mouth unnaturally stiff. She does not know how to be.

In the second photograph, the one you didn't want Martin to take, the woman is clearly annoyed. Her eyes are harder, her lips tight, chin jutting. She looks older, more confident. Formidable even.

I look quite scary.

Even though I'm the one that's frightened.

In the photos, you are smaller than you appear to yourself in the mirror, and paler. Your mother's skin was olive toned. The kind of skin that never looked completely naked, always seemed to be dusted with some expensive translucent powder. You can't imagine that your mother ever had spots as a teenager, or a greasy forehead, or blackheads. Martin's skin is light brown. The hairs on his arms are golden. Your own skin tone is more like your father's; you only have to be a little tired to have dark circles under your eyes.

You remember what Evie said about being beautiful. How will you look back at this girl in twenty years' time? From an imaginary future, you consider her dark hair, almost curling, tied loosely to one side. Her straight shoulders and clear collarbones; the green polo shirt with the nursery logo on the pocket. You study the way her features are placed.

Expressions aside, I look quite nice.

Not beautiful, but healthy.

Even almost pretty.

The sound of a car horn jolts you. You look up to see a woman in a red Fiat next to you, a large blonde woman mouthing a question. She wants your parking space. Are you going? You nod, stuff the photos back into their envelope, shift the car seat forward. As you pull away, you can see her in your rear view mirror. She smiles and waves a thank you.

———

19

You stop at the iron gate for a moment and look up. The house is waiting for you, its red brick and terracotta vibrant in the sunlight. For the first time, you notice a gargoyle under one of the eaves – can't believe you haven't noticed it before – a hunched creature with horns and fangs, a dragon's tail curled to the side. It is smiling down at you. You smile back.

———

Evie says:

I went to an exhibition of paintings. I had not been invited, but there was a sign in the gallery window, so I just went in. And no-one questioned me, which was just as well, my dear, because of course I had no money for an entrance fee. I was nearly eighteen by then, out walking, as was my habit, to escape my father's painful self-pity and the silent dirty house.

'The gallery was very pleasant. There was a woman at a small table near the door, passing out glasses of something bubbly. She smiled – I still remember there was lipstick on her teeth – and she said 'hello' but she didn't offer me a drink. I probably looked too young to drink alcohol. Nevertheless, I smiled back and said 'hello' in a strong, confident voice.

'I had never been in an art gallery before. If you had asked me what I expected, I would have said a large open space with long white walls and bare floors. This was nothing like that; it was a series of small rooms, with the walls and doors painted in warm pastel colours and many pictures displayed on each wall. There was a red carpet on the floor, so thick it seemed to suck up the sound. At first I hovered, pretending to study the pictures.

'I was fascinated by the people there. Some in smart clothes, with beautiful haircuts. Others in cardigans and baggy skirts. It was clear to me that there was no dress code, that being accepted there did not depend on what you wore. It was something else. Some were interested in the art, others paid it no attention whatever, looked a bit bored, even. Some were animated, articulate. Others said nothing. But to my eyes, everyone there looked perfectly confident.

'I know better now, of course. None of them had any real confidence. They were all trying to impress one another.

'I stuck to the edges of the rooms, grateful that one could seem to be busy appreciating the art rather than simply at a loss. It was easy to appear interested in the paintings. It came as a surprise to me when I very soon realised that I *was* interested. I thought they were quite extraordinary, full of wonderful bright shimmering colour. Abstract shapes of colour like fish scales in the sun, oil on water, the shine on a peacock's feather. I knew nothing about art, but I loved those formless paintings. I stayed a long time. I walked the whole gallery several times, very slowly. I noticed, eventually, that it had become quiet. That almost everyone else had gone.

'It was then that a man spoke to me. Older than me, quite a bit older. He asked if I liked the work, if I was familiar with the artist. His face was round, his top lip a bit shiny with sweat, and I realized that he was not in the least bit confident. So I felt my back straighten; I was flirtatious. I looked him in the eyes – he had pale green eyes with light lashes – and spoke to him with the total attention that even then I knew was necessary to draw people in. I used the voice I had developed for just such an occasion, and he never heard me speak any other way.

'He had patches of skin that were red and raised, not eczema, not as persistent as that. Just anxious unsettled patches that he rubbed absentmindedly, on his neck and the inside of his wrists. I learned later that they came up when he was upset or embarrassed. But as we spoke, he relaxed, the patches faded; he was friendly and kind. He asked me to have a drink with him, and then dinner after that.'

Evie opens her eyes. 'You may have guessed, my dear, that this was Harold.'

She sips her lemonade and is quiet. You are not ready for her to stop.

'Tell me more about him,' you say. 'What was he like?'

She says:

'Harold had the extraordinary ability to make even the most expensive suit look like something borrowed. There was nothing about him to suggest strength of character. Not his light eyes and hair, nor his soft, soft skin. Although his whiskers grew very quickly, thick and bristly, slightly ginger.

'Harold had small hands, with small, shiny shell-like fingernails. And he was always stroking or picking at the fabric of something, at the edge of a pocket or a seam in his clothing or the upholstery. He would slide textured fabrics like tweed between his finger and thumb. Constantly. And he was unaware he was doing it. When it got on my nerves, and I told him, he never failed to be surprised; he was embarrassed and apologetic. Then he'd be at it again within ten minutes.

'Harold was very rich. But to be truthful, even the way he had made all his money was rather dull. He was an engineer of some kind. He invented something small but absolutely essential – some kind of nut or bolt that was better than other kinds. It was used in factories all around the world and made him a fortune.

'He bought me this house, you know. For no other reason

than that I wanted it. I didn't care that it was ridiculously big for us. I used to have parties, invited dozens of people I hardly knew, had the best food, the best musicians, the most stylish people. He gave me everything I wanted.

'But I never shared a bed with Harold. I never had any kind of sexual intimacy with him. He knew that was the arrangement and he never questioned it. On occasion, I would allow him to watch me dress. He liked women's clothing, you see. Not in any perverse way; he appreciated the styles and colours of women's fashion. In a different time, a different place, he could have been a designer, some kind of artist perhaps...'

Evie's voice trails off. She takes another sip of her juice.

'The truth is,' she resumes. 'I had real affection for Harold. Grace belittled him, laughed at his slowness and his willingness to please. And we both understood that he was a man who enjoyed being taken advantage of. That he got a kind of satisfaction from being treated badly, in subtle ways. But I liked him.'

She smiles.

'And that's all for now, dear. I'll tell you more another time.'

———

Walking back to the station, you pass a group of foreign students from the language school up the road. You stand back, press against the scented branches of a conifer hedge as the teenagers flow by like a wave; the sound of them swirls around you. They are speaking Spanish or Portuguese; and because you don't understand what they are saying, you notice how they are saying it, the energy behind the words. They are animated, loud, their sentences broken up by laughter. They are a pack, sharing an adventure. They are joyful.

As their chatter recedes, you notice that your own mouth is shaped into a smile, a mirror for theirs. You walk on, leaving the warm shade of the pavement to cross the avenue and waiting in the open sunlight for the traffic lights to change.

Evie doesn't need to be part of a pack. She doesn't require approval. When she is telling her story, you never get the feeling she is colouring what she says to make her behaviour more acceptable to you. Nor do you get the impression that she censors herself.

It's not that she forgets you are there. Her eyes are closed, but she is aware of you listening. Sometimes she is silent for long moments, searching herself for pictures, memories, feelings. Then she shifts focus again, shares them with you, and moves on.

You turn into the shade of the station, walk up the steps and over to the platform on the far side. You find a free bench. The air smells of heat and coffee, dusty machinery.

Today, as she reached the end of her latest chapter, Evie had smiled. No matter how serious, how delicate or how revealing the story, she is enjoying it enormously.

The bench is warm beneath you; you drift; you see:

> *A candlelit room, elegant people at glittering tables. Evie is whispering something into the ear of her companion, a woman who is looking down; you can't see her face. But you can see she is holding Evie's hand in her silky lap, stroking Evie's palm with her thumb.*
>
> *Harold is sitting opposite them. He is watching the two women; he is picking at the seam of his napkin with a forefinger. Still watching, he swirls the liquid and ice in his drink, raises it to his lips and swallows. Then he looks away, seems interested in people on the other side of the room.*
>
> *When the women giggle, Harold looks back and smiles, as though he were included in the joke.*

Doors slam on the train at another platform; an announcement echoes over the loudspeaker; someone shouts. Still wrapped in the rare net of understanding that Evie has woven with you, you are undisturbed.

—

20

The tools are stored in the workshop at the far end of the nursery. They hang here, all shapes and sizes, on hooks and nails that have been banged into the walls as required.

It's a quirky building, three of the walls are solid, brick-built. But the front wall is made entirely of old doors, some with glass panes, others wood-panelled, their letterboxes and keyholes still strangely welcoming. Every year, a stubborn bramble grows in through a broken catflap, the fresh tendrils thriving in the protected conditions, even producing a tiny crop of blackberries in late summer. Every year, you cut it back.

You come in here to brush the dirt off your tools and wipe them with an oily cloth before hanging them up. It is always quiet; you enjoy the feeling of being alone and enclosed. But today you push open the door to find Martin already here, emptying a dirty cardboard box onto the workshop table, making a pile of rusty old tools. You recognise a scythe, hand forks and trowels, shears. Others, you don't recognise at all. Every one of them is corroded in shades of orange and brown, and is, in your eyes, entirely useless.

He holds up a miniature hoe like a rust-encrusted wand.

'Onion hoe,' he announces. Then he moves onto the next item, a prong of ancient metal, and waves that at you.

'Daisy grubber.'

Approaching the bench and looking more closely, you can see that some of the tools in the pile no longer even have handles; the wood has rotted away. Martin is gloating over them.

'Where did you get all this stuff?' you ask.

'Car boot sale.'

'I've never seen anyone look quite so impressed with a pile of rubbish,' you say, poking with a careful fingertip at the oxidised flakes on one unidentifiable metal shape.

'It might look like rubbish now,' he replies. 'But every one of these old tools can be restored back to its former glory.'

He puts the daisy grubber down and picks up something you've never seen before. Wood-handled, with a short metal arm ending in a double blade.

'Look at this.' He exhibits the thing to you like it's a prize in a game show. 'A hundred years old, this is, at least. And with a bit of loving care, it'll be as good as new.'

'That's fantastic,' you say. 'Because the world definitely needs another one of those things.'

You wait, but he says nothing.

'Okay,' you say. 'I give up. What is it?'

'This, my dear woman, is a ringbarking tool.'

You wait for more.

'It strips a ring of bark off a tree,' he explains. 'The nutrients travel up the trunk just under the bark, right? So if you remove a ring of bark, even a narrow one - ' he measures an inch in the air with his free finger and thumb, ' – the nutrients can't get up the tree and it dies.'

'It's a tree killer, then?'

'Yes.'

'Charming.'

He puts the ringbarker down and turns to a bundle of long-handled tools leaning against the wall behind him, selects a rusty hoe with only half a handle.

'The design of these things hasn't really changed since ancient Egypt,' he says. 'Isn't that amazing?' He strokes the wood of the handle. 'I bet this one has been used by generations of gardeners.'

You pull out one of the old wooden chairs leaning against the wall and sit astride it, your arms resting along its back, your chin resting on your arms. You watch as he rummages through the pile, sorting the tools into different categories.

'Martin.'

'Um.'

He wipes his forehead, leaving a streak of red dirt across damp golden skin.

'Would you ever marry for money?'

He looks up, grins at you.

'I might. Who's asking?'

You roll your eyes.

'No, seriously, would you?'

He stops what he's doing. Thinks. Frowns.

'Seriously? No.'

He picks up a piece of wire wool and starts scrubbing at a rusty trowel.

—

21

'**Y**ou never told me how you met Grace Cullen,' you say.

She tells you:

'I discovered Grace soon after I met Harold, before he and I were married. She was present at our wedding. And when Harold bought me this house, she helped me redecorate it in the peacock colours I had seen at the gallery and loved so much.

'Grace Cullen was everything I wanted to be. She was beautiful in a way that I never was. She was glamorous, like the women in the glossy magazines; she was effortlessly confident. She spent a great deal of time here. We would talk for hours, until late, until we fell asleep. Eventually, it seemed entirely natural that she would stay. There was no need for her to leave.'

You sense the quick scrape of something metallic, the taste of iron under your tongue.

Jealousy again.

You sneak a glance at Evie's face. Her eyes are only half closed; she is smiling as she unwraps the memory.

'It was a remarkable time. I didn't love Harold, of course. I was fond of him, and grateful. But I was passionate about Grace. And with her, there was nothing I couldn't do. We went everywhere – to the theatre, to concerts, to fine restaurants. To shabby hotel bars, dark clubs, small private cinema houses to watch foreign films with men. We wanted to do everything, try everything. We had endless discussions about how to amuse ourselves. We were both hugely interested in how people could be understood. Or, more frankly, how they could be manipulated. And that led to enormous fun. To our most ambitious and exciting project.'

She breaks into a grin. You notice for the hundredth time how beautifully her mouth is shaped. Even now, as an old woman, there is something sensual about the way her lips move; even the lines at the corners of her mouth are drawn in clear, confident strokes. There is nothing accidental about Evie's face. You get the sense that she has created it herself, deliberately, over the years.

'Still interested?' she checks playfully, knowing full well that you are.

You nod.

'Excellent,' she smiles. Then she looks past you to one of the crammed bookshelves.

'Could you fetch that box for me, my dear? The purple one?'

It takes you a minute to locate the box she wants amongst the jumble of books and ornaments. It's about the size of a biscuit tin, but not tin, hexagonal, made of papier maché and highly lacquered. Purple patterned in gold.

You pick it up.

'I wasn't expecting it to be that heavy,' you say, as you take it back to the bed.

'Open it,' says Evie. And you do, and it is full of small stones.

'Pebbles,' she says. 'Just ordinary pebbles. But when I chose them off the beach, over fifty years ago, there was something special about each and every one of them. I chose them, one by one, and took them home and they were a kind of treasure to me.'

You pick one out, a smooth grey pebble seamed with white. You test the weight of it in your hand. You see:

A young girl sitting on a beach of pebbles. Eyes closed,

she is running her hands over the stones within her reach, feeling her way with sensitive palms and fingers. Slowly, as if blind, she gathers the shapes and textures into her senses. Then she picks up one pebble, opens her eyes and considers it. She notes the seam of pristine white running through the grey; she touches the smooth surface with her tongue to see the wet colour of it. She chooses it.

'The thing is,' says Evie. 'They were all special once. But they changed. They're ordinary now. Not special at all.' She tilts her head.

'What do you think happened, Claire? Did they simply lose their value, locked away in this box for so long? Did it just drain out of them?'

She raises her eyebrows, but you know you're not expected to respond. You feel your own eyebrows rise slightly, mirroring hers, and wait for her to go on.

'Grace said they never did have any value. That I made them special. Nevertheless, it was these pebbles that inspired her most exciting idea.'

You put the grey stone back in the box; it clicks against the others.

Evie is looking beyond you, out of the window or inwards, you can't tell.

'Do you still miss her?' you ask.

She doesn't reply immediately, doesn't even appear to have heard you. She breathes a long, low sigh, then closes her eyes.

She says:

'Sometimes I can hardly believe that she is gone. It's still so easy to conjure her up. I can see her now, standing naked in front of that mirror. She was beautiful, small and lithe. I loved the muscles in her arms, and the narrow bones of her feet.

'In the mornings, we had coffee at that table, both of us naked. The truth be told, we were naked for much of the time we were in this room. It was a pleasure to come here after being out in the world, to shed our clothes and be totally free of restraints. We loved to sit on the floor in front of the fire, watching the reflection of the flames on each other's skin.

'We were more than close. We slept in this bed, breathing like one person. I knew her thoughts, often, before she spoke them. She knew mine. When she was absent, I felt only half alive.

'Which is not to say that we were similar in all ways. Grace was more extreme than I, less careful. Whereas I might think harsh things but speak tactfully, she would say them outright, careless of whom she hurt. The truth is, I think Grace enjoyed cutting people with her words, slicing off thin slivers that sometimes they didn't even notice.

'And Grace was more demanding than I. Far more demanding. She decided, once, that she wanted to go to dinner at the finest hotel in the town and she demanded that Harold reserve the entire hotel for a night. Not just the restaurant, or even the whole floor. She would not be happy unless he booked the entire hotel, so that it was completely empty except for staff. It took some time to organize. She was very impatient about it. And then, on the evening, with the hotel full of empty rooms and the restaurant open only to us, she decided we weren't going, after all. All that trouble he had gone to, and she just didn't feel like going.

'Really, her extravagance was shocking. When we shopped, she would insist that everything I had was unique, made especially for me, in a range of colours. It was more than I could ever hope to wear. The most extraordinary dresses, couture gowns, would pile up here, many never even taken out of the tissue paper they were wrapped in.

'Looking back, it's hard to believe that Harold went along with it all. But I think he would have done anything to make me happy. He never said anything against Grace.

'And for her part, most of the time, Grace hardly acknowledged he was there. Occasionally, she was cruel to him. She told him how close we were; she knew it would hurt him. But she also knew that there was something in him that liked to be hurt. Sometimes, she left our bedroom door open, a deliberate gap for him to see through if he passed by.'

Evie opens her eyes and regards you steadily, head tilted to one side.

'I don't know if he ever did.'

—

22

The sunshine is fuzzy and gentle, it settles like powder on the shapes and angles of the gathered things on your kitchen table.

You sit in one of the wooden kitchen chairs, the old cushion lumpy underneath you. It's quiet. There is no clock in here to measure out the seconds; time could be stretching, contracting, standing still for all you know.

Grace had known Evie when she was young, before she was ill, when she was passionate and available. Grace had been her accomplice, her beloved.

You pick up a tiny grey paper ball, the beginnings of a wasps' nest; you had discovered it in the outside cupboard and removed it before the colony could grow large enough to be a problem. The paper is tough and malleable. Like manmade paper, it is made of wood; the wasps have chewed it into paste, fashioned it into thin curved layers. You hold it in the palm of your hand for a moment, wondering where the queen relocated her fledgling colony after you stole their nest. You put it back into the bowl.

You would have hated Grace Cullen. She had been cruel, selfish and manipulative. She hadn't deserved Evie's love. Not like you would have done.

See:

Yourself, sitting opposite a young Evie at the kitchen

table. She is alert, upright, completely well – the young woman you have seen in photographs. Her eyes hold yours as she reaches across the table and with one hand turns your hand palm up, and with one fingertip traces the blue veins of your inside wrist.

See:

A small shop, expensive, select. There are no other customers, just an attentive shop assistant with her hair in angular lines, high cheekbones, sleek lapels. You are sitting on a small sofa, curved and hard with a buttoned back. Evie steps out of the changing room. Slender, straight Evie, in a gown of raw silk. She laughs, twirls, looking over her shoulder at you, and the seagreen material rustles around her.

See:

Evie, standing in front of the long mirror in a dress of exquisite sequins. The shadowy figure of a woman lying on the bed, watching.

Evie pirouettes, laughs, then unzips the gown and lets it fall into a shining mess around her feet.

She steps out of it and jumps squealing onto the bed where you are waiting.

———

– *23* –

Evie says:

'We wanted to do something unusual and a bit risky. Something that both challenged and entertained us. Grace was looking at the box of stones I showed you, the purple box, when she had the idea.

'She decided I would become a reader of stones. Not runes – nothing as overtly mystical as that. Ordinary stones. Pebbles from the beach or the garden.

'The idea was this: that if a person carried a stone for twenty-four hours, it would absorb their aura, their energetic field. And that simply by holding it, I could read whatever truth that person needed to know. It sounds silly now, telling you about it. I thought it was silly at the time, that it would never work. But it was Grace's idea, and Grace was never wrong. She was cleverer than I, she had the ability to look far ahead, to create schemes and plans that allowed for every contingency.

'Well, this wonderful new idea started quietly enough. Grace spoke to one or two of the wealthy ladies she knew, let it be known that she had come across someone with a real gift. Yes, she said, she might be able to arrange something. Possibly. She would have a word. In the meantime, she told them, find a pebble you're drawn to, and keep it with you.

'They came to see me in a suite in a quiet hotel. They were never disappointed. They told their friends. Appointments were only ever made by word of mouth, by recommendation.'

Evie's voice chimes with quiet self-satisfaction.

You see:

Evie, young and upright, wearing jade silk, waiting on an elegant chair in an expensive room. Sunlight slices through a tall window, glances off her cheekbones, reveals the skin around her eyes as smooth as rice paper. She rises to greet a visitor, speaks with quiet confidence. She holds out her hand, receives the small stone.

Rather than closing her fingers around it, she covers the pebble gently with her other hand, like a woman holding a butterfly. She sits, silent and serious. Her visitor shifts nervously. Then Evie smiles, that astonishing smile that invites you into the light of her eyes, and the visitor is relieved, charmed, bends forward closely to hear her quiet words.

'Of course, I only saw people who had a lot of money, but there was never a set fee. That would have been too crass. Grace told them I would be happy with a small donation, whatever felt appropriate – and nothing at all if the subject felt unsatisfied with the reading. Eventually she let it be known that we were raising funds to establish an institution of some kind, and we received some very large sums of money indeed. We didn't need it, of course. We just loved the power of it. We rushed through those days on a wave of excitement. Yes, it really was a wonderful time.'

She blinks then, as if awakening, regards you from her pillows. 'If you're wondering what I told them,' she says, 'It was only what they wanted to hear. That they were deeply special in some way. That they deserved love and appreciation. That their true talents had not yet been recognized. It's not difficult to manipulate people, my dear.'

At the end of her bed, legs pulled up beneath you, you stretch and roll your shoulders to ease the muscles.

'It can't really be that easy,' you say. 'Or everyone would do it.'

'But it can, my dear. There are seven rules. Let me tell you:

'One. Show them you understand – better than anyone – just how sensitive they are, how deeply they have been hurt.

She nods wisely to demonstrate understanding.

'Two. Be entranced by them, make their ordinariness extraordinary.

She raises her eyebrows.

'Three. Lead them to believe they have a unique relationship with you. Tell them secrets.

Another serious nod.

'Four. Praise them for all the attributes you wish them to have – they will not want to disappoint you.

She tilts her head, expectant.

'Five. Repeat exactly what they tell you, using different words; they will feel deeply understood.

She winks.

'And six. Be silent sometimes – people value your words more if there are times when you say nothing.

She smiles brightly.

'Finally,' she says, 'Seven. Keep an eye on the balance of give and take; notice when you need to give something, to take something, so there is the semblance of equality between you.'

She laughs then, and it is the sound of playful water over broken glass.

'Why are you telling me all this, Evie? Things that might make me think less of you?'

'What you must understand, my dear, is that every story craves to be told. If I don't tell you my story fully and honestly, it will always try and find its way out; it will never lie still.'

Her eyes are clear, gentle.

'And, of course, I trust you not to judge me too harshly.'

You rest in her gaze for a second or two, then point to the purple box.

'Are some of those the stones that you read for people?'

'No, dear. I made people take their own stones home with them,' she smiles broadly. 'In fact, I made each of them feel it was a gift. They were grateful. Imagine that.'

She twinkles at you.

—

'**D**o you know anything about cameras?'

Martin is shifting a trolley-load of shrubs from the back yard out onto display. He stops, wipes his forehead with his arm, wipes his hands on his jeans.

'God, it's hot. What was that, Claire?'

'I was just wondering,' you say. 'Do you know anything about cameras?' You lean against a fence post. The sun has soaked into the timber; its warmth seeps out into your back.

'Not a lot,' he says. 'A bit. What kind of photos do you want to take?'

'Close-ups. Really close details of things.'

'You'll need a good zoom, then. Best thing would be to ask in a camera shop. They'll tell you exactly what you need.'

You feel yourself shrinking, daunted by the prospect of technical things, of speaking to a clever salesman about something you don't understand.

'What's the matter?' Martin has read your expression.

'No, nothing,' you say. 'I was just hoping you might know... that you might be able to tell me. So I could just go in and ask for it.'

'I could come with you, if you like,' he says.

'No,' you answer, too quickly. 'It's okay, I can do it.'

'Okay.'

You scuff the back of your heel against the fencepost.

'What's brought this on?' he asks. 'The sudden interest in photography?'

He is curious. You have his full attention.

'When you took those snapshots of me the other week, remember? We only took two pictures. So I used up the rest of the film, but the pictures didn't come out very well.' You shrug. 'I don't know. I just want to take some better pictures.'

> *I want to open a window into a place where colours are like jewels.*

> *I want to make small things so big they become a whole world.*

> *I want to surround myself in a peel of bark. Wrap myself in a leaf. See the moss like a forest.*

> *I want an ant-sized view.*

Martin is standing with his hands on his hips, head tilted, observing you.

'Well, there's a good camera shop at the bottom of Trafalgar Street. And if you change your mind,' he says, 'I'd be happy to come along.'

He turns his attention back to the trolley, heads off towards the front of the nursery. You watch him go, measuring the seconds in the bouncing of the wire basket, the rattling of the wheels on the uneven path. A sense of loss rolls through you, intensifies as Martin moves away. The loss of exquisite pictures you haven't yet taken, revelations of small things made large. You open your mouth, still unsure you will say anything, but your throat releases his name.

'Martin!'

He stops, turns, waits.

'I've changed my mind,' you say. 'I'd like to go to the camera shop with you. Soon. Okay?'

'Okay.' He grins. Rattles off with the trolley.

You feel something release and relax within you. Like you have been holding on tightly and have just let go. You tighten your fist, hard, until it is uncomfortable. Then you let go, feel the gentle swell of blood pulsing in your palm, and the sense that your fingers are floating.

Yes. You feel just like that.

———

– 25 –

It still feels strange, letting yourself in. The new key is stiff in the Yale lock but the heavy door glides open for you; the house ushers you in. You run up the stairs, arrive breathless outside Evie's door, tap gently.

'Do come in, Claire.'

She's not alone. Margaret has just changed a pillowcase, is arranging the pillows around Evie's head. You stand at the foot of the bed, still catching your breath, but you can't wait to tell Evie about your plans to get a camera.

'Guess what?' you say, too loudly.

They both look up at you. Heads close together, eyes on your face, they both look up.

And you see.

That Margaret's eyes are a darker shade of brown, puffier, the eyelids fleshier. That Evie's are older, more refined. That, in spite of these differences, their eyes are exactly the same shape. Large and deep under finely drawn brows. Separately, you would never have noticed. But together, so close, you see.

You forget about the camera, caught up in this new train of thought, looking from one face to the other, searching for further similarities.

Evie's eyes narrow. But Margaret is oblivious, impatient.

'What?' she says. 'What?'

Still you say nothing, your eyes on Evie now, hers on you. Margaret pats crossly at the pillow, straightens up. She is offended. She thinks you don't want to speak to Evie in front of her.

'I'll leave you to it then.' She stomps out.

You stand at the foot of the bed, facing Evie across the curved wooden footboard.

'Margaret is your daughter.'

You have to push the words out; you forgot to take a breath before speaking.

'Yes.'

'The one you gave up for adoption.'

'Yes.'

'Does she know?'

'Of course not, my dear. All things considered, I very much doubt she'd be pleased about it.'

You rub your hands over your face, feeling the tug of muscle over bone, the pull of skin under your fingers, the heat of your flushed cheeks.

I can't believe this.

But you can. Easily, you can. It has always been in Evie's voice, along with the disdain. A note of ownership.

That child will always be mine. She belongs to me and she will be mine until the day she dies.

'The way you speak to her, Evie. And about her. As though you hate her. And she's your *daughter*.'

'Don't be so shocked, Claire darling. It doesn't suit you.'

'But you told me – '

'I told you she had been adopted. And that was entirely true. I just didn't tell you the rest.'

She pauses, opens her eyes wide as if to say, 'See? I haven't misled you at all.'

All at once you want to sit down, but not on the end of her bed. You sink into the brown brocade chair.

'The fact is,' she goes on, 'After Harold died, and then

Grace left, it was a terribly lonely time. I wanted to feel connected to someone.'

She is entirely serious now.

'I commissioned a private investigator to look for her. He found her. And as it happens, she wasn't that far away. She was only a little girl then, and there was nothing I could do to change the situation at that point. Indeed, there was nothing I wanted to do; I had no real desire to be the parent of a small child. So I watched her grow up, from a distance.

'Over the years, I received regular reports, what she was doing, how well she was performing at school, whether she was healthy. I daresay I knew nearly as much about her as her adoptive family.'

You see:

> *Younger Evie, opening the door to the house, taking a large envelope from the man on the doorstep. Back into the house, in the kitchen, she puts the envelope down on the big kitchen table, sits in front of it. She opens the envelope, takes out a bundle of papers and separates the different documents out in front of her on the table. Then she reads until the afternoon light fades. And then she sits, eyes closed, holding the last page on her lap as the room grows dark around her.*

She clears her throat, as if she has noticed that you are not listening. When you nod, she goes on.

'When Margaret turned twenty-one, I wrote to her through a solicitor, using my maiden name. I asked her to meet me.'

Evie is looking past you, over your shoulder, remembering. Her face tightens, the bottom lip juts, her chin ripples. You see something you have never seen before – that Evie is capable of something more violent that disdain. For a moment, she looks almost ugly.

'And?' you prompt her.

'And she refused. Wrote a brief letter saying that she was

happy and would I please leave her be.'

She inhales deeply, pulls her mouth into a smile again.

'I was upset, as you can imagine. I didn't know her then, and I honestly imagined that there might be some kind of a bond between us. Of course that's ludicrous, I know that now. But I could have given her a wonderful life; she could have had anything she wanted. And the silly fool said no.'

'But she's here now,' you say. 'How did you manage that?'

'Patience, Claire. I haven't told anyone about this before. Let me tell it in my own way.' She has regained some of her poise, sounds almost amused now.

'I retained the services of the investigator. So I knew when Margaret got married, and when she had a child, a boy, terribly handicapped. Oh dear, that's not the right word to use these days, is it? But you know my meaning. I knew about it when her adoptive father died. And when her husband started an affair – in fact I knew about that before she did. And when he left her, I knew where he had gone.'

She turns her head and sips lemonade, taking her time.

'When her adoptive mother died, some years later, I wrote to her again. And that time I got no response at all. Looking back now I can't imagine what kept me so interested. Her life, I assure you, was anything but interesting. By that time, her child had grown into an adult, she had had to put him into a care home, not a very good one. She was working, doing something horribly menial, very low paid. Struggling to meet the costs, even though he wasn't being well cared for.'

You remember how Margaret's chin had wobbled as she told you about her son, explained why she continued working for Evie. Why hadn't you felt more sympathy for her then? Something unpleasant is growing in your chest, spreads like a stain.

I am ashamed of myself.

Evie is not. She is thoroughly enjoying sharing her cleverness with you. Her eyes gleam as she lays it out in front of you.

'I had a lot of time to think, over the years,' she says. 'And I hatched a plan. It was very simple really, my dear. I bought the nursing home where her son was living, I made some significant improvements and increased the fees. She must have been at her wits' end, worrying how she was going to afford the increase, where else he could go. Until I engineered a job offer, a live-in position looking after the rich old woman who owned the home; it was a position that enabled her son to stay where he was, and receive even better care.'

Evie's eyes crease as she smiles; she is apparently still immensely satisfied with the success of her plan.

'Of course she accepted the offer. She had no reason to believe I was the woman who had given birth to her.'

'But why did you bother, Evie? Why go to so much trouble to find her, to trick her into living under your roof?'

Evie sighs.

'To be totally honest, my dear, I'm not entirely sure. Perhaps, after everything, I was still hoping for something good to come out of it. Some kind of relationship, once she had a chance to know me, and I her.'

Her mouth tightens again.

'But she has disappointed me, Claire. No matter how hard I look, there is nothing exceptional in her. Nothing of myself.'

You can feel your own eyes narrow as you weigh up her words.

'What are you going to do now, Evie? Are you going to tell her?'

'Why? Because you've put two and two together? Of course not, my dear. I see absolutely no reason to upset the apple cart at this late stage.'

She is so beautiful. This silver haired woman with the delightful smile, the engaging eyes.

'It will be our secret,' she twinkles at you.

'It's not my secret, Evie,' you say. 'It's yours.'

'Remember, Claire – she didn't want to know me when she had the chance.'

This is wrong. Margaret should know.

You feel the certainty of that like a solid weight in the pit of your stomach. But Evie's smile, her affectionate conspiracy, are relentless. You can't imagine speaking against her wishes.

'I won't say anything,' you tell her.

'Good. Now go, please, dear. I'm tired.'

———

You take the longer way back to the station, past the shops. A woman is hanging shoes in one of the windows. Glittering grccn cvening shoes; sandals with silver straps; red shoes with buttons. She is standing in the window suspending each shoe from a length of fishing line so it seems to float. An old man stands outside the window, watching, nodding and smiling, clapping as each shoe is hung. You wait for him to fade, to disappear. He turns, sees you.

'What will they think of next? Shoes flying in a window, that's what!'

His laugh is light and high, but real. He is not a ghost. You smile weakly and walk around him.

———

26

Home.

You make tea, take your mug down the path through the garden, weaving amongst the brambles to the stream at the back. It's only a shallow stream but over the years it has worn through the soft earth to a bed of stones a couple of feet below the bank. To dip your fingers in the water, you have to lie on your stomach and lean over the edge. You haven't done that since you were a child.

Now you sit cross-legged in the rough grass and ferns, under an ash tree with naked roots twisted into the bank. The water is strangely silent, so sure of its way it slips over the familiar stones without making a sound. In the evening, the midges will irritate, sliding into your eyes. But now, in the heat of the afternoon, they are still.

Evie is Margaret's mother.

You are gripping your mug too hard; you put it down, press it firmly into the ground so it won't fall over. Your forehead creases, aches.

Evie. Margaret's mother.

You place your palm on your forehead, close your eyes. You haven't been able to dislodge the image in your mind of

Evie's face, the unfamiliar ugliness of it, when she spoke about Margaret's rejection. You have never seen anything like violence in Evie's features before. This was pure hatred.

That's what it would take. To keep that secret, day after day, over the years.

You feel pressure at the back of your throat, as if you could be physically sick.

Then there is Margaret, blundering around the massive house, manufacturing a sense of justice out of small acts of spite. Pitiful, lumpy Margaret. So completely outmatched by the woman in the bed upstairs. See:

Margaret's broad face quivering with emotion as she sits with you in the kitchen.

'Evie pays for my son to be looked after. Somewhere good and safe, where the staff can be trusted to treat him well.'

What would Margaret do if she discovered Evie was using her son to manipulate her, to play games with her life? Margaret is already sullen and resentful; what might her anger become if she knew?

Heavy and rough, like a blunt saw.

You feel the scrape of anxiety even before the thought rises into consciousness.

If Margaret knew, could Evie be in real danger?

Something is pressing into your thigh, a stick or a rock. You uncross your legs, stretch them out in front of you.

Perhaps Margaret is better off not knowing. Her son will remain well looked after. And if she doesn't get on with Evie; well. Lots of people don't like their employers...

That train of thought stalls, falls apart. The crease in your forehead deepens.

It's wrong.

I should tell Margaret.

You pick up your tea, fish out a floating grass seed before swallowing a lukewarm mouthful.

But if I tell Margaret, I will have to leave.

There is no doubt in your mind; Evie would not tolerate disloyalty. You can hear the disappointment in her voice: *Your services are no longer required, Claire. I can no longer trust you.* You can see her turn her head aside on the pillow, silently waiting for you to go.

You don't want to leave.

You can't tell Margaret.

You pick up your mug again, tip the cold tea onto the earth at the base of the tree, watch as it soaks into the ground. It is cool here in the shade, but there's a warm patch on your shoulder where the sun is slipping through a gap in the branches. You shut your eyes, feel the patch of warmth as intensely as you can.

There is a plopping sound from the stream. As a child, you believed that if you were fast enough, you could catch sight of whatever it was that did that. But no matter how quickly you turned your head, there was never anything to be seen, no frog, no fish, nothing to explain the sound. Now, you resist the temptation to check. You take a deep breath, allowing the air to expand your ribs, breathe out as slowly as you can, feeling your lungs deflate, your bones settle.

What would Grace have done?

Grace would have joined Evie in the game. She would have taken part in the plotting, the planning. You envy Grace.

But I don't want to be like her.

I am not like Grace.

Something rustles in the bushes to your left. A bird. A rat. You imagine small naked paws, translucent claws.

If you carry on seeing Evie, knowing what you know, you will be her accomplice. The crease in your forehead is becoming a headache behind your right eye.

It might be best if I just don't go back. I could tell the woman from Probation that it hasn't worked out. That I want to complete my community sentence doing something else.

Imagine:

Not waking up knowing you will be seeing Evie.

Not feeling the thread of connection between you.

Not doing everything slowly, enjoying each step towards being with her.

Instead, on the days that are no longer Evie's, there will be the hollowness of going-through-the-motions. Eating your cereal standing up, looking out the kitchen window at the hedge, checking the bird feeder, measuring the strength of the wind by the movement of the trees.

Already you feel the twist of grief. The sense of going back to being only half alive.

I don't like what Evie is doing.

But I love Evie.

You stand up, hold onto the narrow trunk of the tree and lean out over the stream. Things show themselves more clearly through water. Even the mud and stones of the streambed look beautiful through it.

A winged insect passes near your head; its drone rises and falls, rises and disappears.

I don't have to approve of what she is doing.

I just have to live with it until I can convince her it's wrong; that she should tell Margaret the truth.

A ripple of relief passes through you. This is the solution.

On some level, you recognize you have made a bargain, and that it is not entirely honourable. But this is how you can keep seeing Evie.

Not this week, though.

You won't go back this week. You have to let Evie know that you disapprove.

You pick up your mug, walk back to the house.

—

27

It's a narrow shop; you've never noticed it before. Inside, it goes back a long way with a counter running the full length of one side and display cases on the other. Everything is silver, grey or black. Nothing attracts you. The sleek contours of technology do not interest you – there is nothing organic or beautiful about it. You stand in front of a display case, completely at a loss.

'See anything you like?' asks Martin.

'No. But I don't need to like it, do I? I just need to be able to take the pictures I want to take.' You turn to him and raise your hands (I give up), 'And I have no idea which one of these will do that.'

Martin grins at you. 'Let's ask someone for help then, shall we?'

He looks different in this environment. Smaller. Wirier. More obviously someone who spends his time outdoors. In cotton t-shirt and jeans, his body is slender and hard. The man behind the counter is heavy, pale, with dark curly hair, dark eyebrows. His badge tells you he is Joe, Manager.

'What do you want the camera for?' he asks Martin.

Martin looks at you.

'I'd like to take close-up photos,' you say. 'That's all, really. I like details...' You trail off.

Martin looks back at Joe.

'And how much do you want to spend?' This time Joe asks you directly.

'Not too much,' you say. 'I'm not even sure I'll be able to get the hang of it.'

It seems that this is all Joe needs to know. He opens up a display case, picks up two small squarish cameras, places them in front of you on the counter. He opens another cabinet, adds one more to the selection.

'Any one of these will give you good quality close-ups,' he says. 'They have great optical zoom...' he reads the look on your face and stops, points with a blunt finger. 'This one.' The silver one. 'Is probably the easiest to use. Good battery life too.'

He takes a photo of the zip on a camera case to demonstrate, shows you the picture on the display. You can see the little nylon teeth in perfect clarity, locking into one another. The stitching. The gaps between the stitches. You begin to feel excited.

Joe shows you how, and you take a close-up shot of the edge of the counter, even manage to capture the smear of a fingerprint.

'This will be fine,' you say.

When you pay for the camera, you don't get the one you've been practising with. Joe gives you a new one in a box. You won't be able to use it until you have charged the battery. On the way home, you look at everything as if it's a potential close-up. The dashboard of the Land Rover. The buckle on your bag. Martin's cheek.

'Thanks, Martin,' you say. 'For taking me. For helping me choose.'

He glances over at you, smiles.

Watching his profile, you notice how relaxed he looks; his mouth and the line of his jaw is easy. He is driving through the tunnel of leaves on the way back to the nursery, the sun is brilliant at the other end. He looks happy.

You imagine a similar feeling of contentment building in you. Your own face would relax. You would shut your eyes for a moment and enjoy the play of light and shade on your face, the sudden wash of warmth as the Land Rover emerges out of the tunnel into the sunlight.

But it isn't like that. Now that the excitement of choosing the camera is over, you have reconnected with the heaviness that has been with you since you guessed Evie's secret, and the anxiety of missing a visit today.

You have never missed a visit before. In the end, you couldn't bear the idea of letting her expect you and just not turning up, so you had called Margaret to let her know you weren't coming.

'Margaret. It's me, Claire.'

'Yes, hello.' Her voice was flat, uninterested.

'Could you tell Evie that I can't make it today, please?'

'Yes. Should I tell her why?'

'No thank you. Just say I'll see her next week.'

Now you wonder exactly what Margaret would have said to Evie, whether she would even have told her at all. You wonder what it had been like for Evie, to be disappointed.

You see:

> *Margaret answering Evie's call bell. Standing in the doorway, heavy, waiting for her to speak.*
>
> *'Claire is late,' says Evie. 'That's not like her. Do you think she's alright?'*
>
> *'She's not coming this week,' says Margaret. 'Sorry, forgot to tell you.' Her mouth is stretched into a smirk as she turns away and goes back downstairs.*

You see:

> *Margaret knocking on Evie's door, popping her head into the room.*
>
> *'Claire just called. She can't come today.'*

'What? Speak clearly, Margaret. Come in and try not to mumble.'

'Claire says she can't come today, she'll see you next week.'

Evie's eyes narrow. She says nothing, and Margaret turns to leave. As she goes, Evie says 'You've spilt something down your top, Margaret. Change it, please.'

Martin is humming under his breath, his hands tapping the steering wheel like a drum. You wonder what it would be like to tell him.

I have discovered that Evie's housekeeper is her daughter. That she keeps it a secret. That she's playing some horrible kind of game.

You know you can't do that. It would be disloyal to Evie, a breach of confidence.

And it shows Evie in a bad light. I want Martin to think well of her.

You won't tell Martin. Not yet. In time, everything could change. The fact that you know the truth now – that Evie has finally spoken about it – might be a catalyst. It could still work out for the best.

The Land Rover slows and Martin turns into the nursery, the thick tyres crunch over the gravel. He switches off the engine and the two of you sit, listening to the ticking of the cooling metal, looking across the field next to the greenhouses.

'Do you ever have recurring dreams?' asks Martin. 'The same one, over and over again?''

'I know what recurring means,' you say.

'Well, do you?'

'Um.' You picture the slow surge of murky water, grey fishskin. Martin is watching your face.

'I dream about fish quite a lot, underwater things.'

'Nice.'

'No.' You shake your head. 'They aren't nice fish. They're all either ill or sad or dangerous.'

You resist the urge to shut down the conversation or take it in another direction.

'The water isn't even clean,' you say. 'They can't see where they're going. What I'd really love is to have recurring dreams about bright shiny fish in very clear water.'

You turn towards him.

'What about you? Do you have any recurring dreams?'

He is still watching your face, his blue eyes honest, unguarded.

'I sometimes dream that I'm looking for something I can't find,' he says. 'But it's never exactly the same dream. Sometimes I'm looking for a place, other times it's something really ordinary like a spade. Sometimes I don't even know what it is. But the feeling is always the same – it always feels incredibly important.'

He looks at you, the sun washing his face in light.

'What I'd really love, just once, is to have a dream that lets me find whatever the hell it is I'm looking for.' Then he smiles, opens the door, jumps out onto the noisy gravel.

'Come on,' he says. 'Let's make a cup of tea before you go home.'

You follow him, the new camera in its box tucked under your arm.

———

'Do you have any photographs of your mother?' Evie once asked you.

There are some in an old suitcase in the wardrobe in your parents' bedroom. You rarely come in here. It smells stuffy but dry and warm. The windows have been shut all summer, but the patterned curtains are open, so the room is full of light that sinks into the faded cream walls and the cream carpet.

To reach the suitcase, you have to move a cardboard box full of coat hangers, a file full of old bills and bank statements, some old towels. The suitcase is the soft, flat kind with straps and buckles, tartan canvas. The zip is sticky.

There are photos of your mother, of your parents together, of the three of you together. Some are framed but most are still in the cardboard envelopes that came from the developers. One at a time you take them out and display them on the blue wool blanket on top of your parents' bed. Then you step back so you can see all the pictures at once.

The one that stands out, demands to be noticed, is a black and white close-up of your mother. Her eyes are full of humour and intelligence. She is laughing, the corners of her eyes creased. She is totally focused on the lens of the camera, on your father behind the lens.

There is another, of you and your mother together. She has her arm around you; you are both looking at the camera, both smiling. You pick this one up and sit on the edge of the bed, searching her face, then yours. There is nothing in this picture but ease and affection – of the difficult feelings, the resentment, nothing shows.

But did you ever outwardly compete with your mother? Certainly not for your father's attention – you would have had no chance, and you knew it. In the same way you know that, if Grace Cullen were still around, you would not challenge her for Evie's attention.

But you competed with your mother in other ways. Knowing the Latin names for plants; you won at that.

Only because she wasn't interested and didn't even try.

The game your mother liked best was Scrabble. It annoyed her that you didn't take it seriously. Sooner or later, you spoiled the game for her by putting down made-up words.

'Claire, I'm not playing with you because you'll get silly.'

'No Mum, I promise I won't this time. I'll play properly.'

And you would, just long enough for her to get engrossed in

the game. You would watch her narrow her eyes and purse her lips as she thought of the best word, the best placing – her mounting triumph as she added another high score into the notebook. And then you would put down 'stwump' or 'opertit', fizzing with suppressed laughter.

———

You plugged the charger into a socket in your living room. The tiny light blinked green when the battery was fully charged.

The camera is not difficult to use. It can do lots of things you don't understand, but you already know how to do the things you want to do.

There is a magic zoom function. You can put the lens so close to a flower that it is almost touching, and magnify it many times over. You can take a photograph that reveals the character of pollen, the architecture of the petal, the green tones in the white.

Or you can use the ordinary zoom and stand back, holding the camera ready until your arms ache, waiting for a bumblebee to settle. If you time it right, you can capture the treacle-coloured hairs on its legs, the plastic yellow of its pollen panniers, the dense velvet of its body. More often, you catch a brown blur or a streak of shadow as the bee flies out of the frame – or nothing at all. And it doesn't matter. You can take dozens of photos, hundreds. You just delete the ones you don't want.

The camera is a gift. You gave it to yourself. Not a furtive gift like the things you shoplifted. A real gift that you wanted and asked for, gave and received.

———

28

In the woods.

You are placing sticks next to each other in a row on the ground. The ground is uneven and the sticks are not identical; some are curved, some pale, others nearly black. But with enough of them side by side, they become something else; they fit together and create a new thing. Some you break; they snap in the quiet air and you place them in a curve. You like the spacing, the geometry of the sticks as they negotiate the turn. More sticks, and the thing has become a spiral. In its centre there is a space that invites the careful placing of something significant. A small pile of seedheads. An arrangement of fern and feathers.

You leave it empty, keep it as a space.

The light is fading, becoming twilight, your least favourite time of day. You hate the blur between light and dark, the fuzzing of edges, the cottony texture of things. There is a wrongness in the air, as if it is dense with something.

In the woods, twilight is darker than in the open, the shadows are deeper and greener. You take one last look at the spiral of sticks, the space in the centre, then turn and head for home.

———

You move to the end of the bed, sit down without saying anything.

Evie looks pale today, and serious. She is too perceptive to be unaware that your missed visit was a statement of disapproval. And she wouldn't care that you disapproved. But she does care whether you come or not, that much is clear. It occurs to you that she might be angry, might say *don't mess me about, Claire, don't come back again.*

Anxiety stirs in your chest and you spread your hands flat on the bedspread, focus on the smooth-rough-smooth of the velvet under your palms.

Evie waits until you look at her, until you are as quiet and serious as she is, then she speaks with surprising emphasis.

'I'm very glad to see you, Claire.'

At the sound of her voice, you feel a warm stain of pleasure creeping up your neck, and the sting of rising tears.

'I'm glad to see you too,' you say. And you reach out, touch her still hand with your own unsteady fingertips, quickly.

She smiles then, and her whole face lights, becomes beautiful.

'Poor Claire. I have put you in an untenable position, haven't I? You disapprove so completely of my actions, don't you my dear? And I expect you are struggling terribly with how to continue here without seeming to condone what I am doing.'

She is watching your face closely, measuring your feelings, your responses.

'Did you think about staying away for good?' she asks.

You nod.

'I wondered if you would,' she tilts her head. 'And how did you reconcile yourself to coming back?'

You clear your throat. 'I decided I would come back and talk you into changing your mind.'

'I see.' She looks you squarely in the eye. 'And what if I don't, Claire? What if I do not budge?'

'Then... I don't know.'

You bite the inside of your cheek. 'Can you at least think about it, Evie? Can you just try and look at it from Margaret's point of view?'

You see the precise moment when her gaze turns inward to find an answer to your question.

'Yes, I can do that,' she nods.

You realize you have been holding your breath, exhale.

'Shall we leave it at that for now then?' she asks. 'Shall we put it aside, talk again in a couple of months to see if either of us has changed perspective?'

You nod. She smiles.

'The day you didn't come because you were angry with me,' says Evie. 'I missed you, Claire. I missed your presence and your patient listening. It has meant the world to me to be able to talk to you, to tell you the truth of things. And of course, we are at a crucial part of the story. This is something I have carried with me for years and never spoken of, not to anyone.'

Her words are like an embrace. You are a vessel, the container of Evie's story. She is transferring it to you in increments, filling you up with it.

'I'm enjoying it,' you say, and the words are completely inadequate. 'I mean, it's important to me to hear it.'

'Shall I go on, then?'

'Yes, please.'

You settle, use one shoe to squash the back of the other shoe down, press it off, then use the toes of the bare foot to remove the remaining shoe. You rest your back against the foot of the bed, lift your knees sideways, tuck both feet under you.

Evie says:

'I have to tell you how Harold died.'

And then she stops. Looks away from you, around the room, as though she is searching for something. In the silence, the clock is loud and slow. A seagull flaps past the window, there's a single hoarse call and feathers batter the air; you turn towards the window but too late, the square of pale sky is empty. When you turn back, Evie is looking past you.

She says:

'The policeman in charge was suspicious. He came back on several occasions, asked the same questions on each occasion. Where was I when it happened? Was it my habit to go out on my own? Were Harold and I happy in our marriage? He was an ugly man, with a long face and jowls. Grace saw him outside watching the house more than once. But there was nothing he could prove. There was, of course, nothing to prove. It had been an accident. Awful, unforeseen, almost bizarre. But no-one's fault.'

Evie's voice is matter of fact.

'Harold fell down the stairs. He tripped over the cord of his dressing gown, fell and banged his head so hard it caused internal bleeding. I was away that night; only Grace was in the house. She said she heard an awful sound as he fell, then a terrible groan. She said she heard him calling out for help.'

Evie stops speaking, presses her lips together. You wait. She takes a breath.

'Grace said she turned the radio up loud so she couldn't hear.'

You gasp. Not a quick loud gasp but a long slow intake of breath that is almost silent. Evie notices and nods confirmation, yes, it is shocking.

You see:

> *Grace Cullen, sitting on the turquoise sofa in the bedroom, flipping through an expensive magazine. She hears something, goes to the door. She hesitates in the doorway for a few moments, moves out onto the landing.*

> *Grace Cullen stands on the landing, looking up, listening to Harold calling out from the floor above.*

> *Then she turns back to the bedroom, closes the door behind her. She hurries across the room, turns up the radio, picks up her magazine.*

'Eventually,' says Evie, 'Harold's cries for help must have stopped.'

She looks troubled.

'The thing is, my dear, the truth of it is, I will never know whether he could have been saved. Whether, if Grace had called for a doctor, if he had received medical treatment, he would have lived. So I don't even know if what she did was, technically, murder.'

Her face is open and vulnerable.

'I think it was. In my heart of hearts, I know she left him there, unheeded, because she intended for him to die.'

She shakes her head.

'I was very angry with her. We had never even discussed the possibility of removing Harold. Not by any means. I was fond of Harold. And without him, the dynamic between Grace and I was wrong; it was out of balance.

'I discovered very quickly that somehow, it had been Harold who made it safe to be with Grace. His corner of the triangle had been so unassuming; so seemingly passive. And yet without him there to counterbalance Grace's capricious ways, her intensity, I couldn't cope with her. I asked her to leave very soon afterwards.'

Evie sighs.

'So. Then I was alone in this house. I grieved for Harold. He had been laughable, ineffectual in so many ways. But I missed him and I mourned him. Of course, on a financial level I was richer. A great deal richer. As the sole beneficiary of Harold's will, I became very wealthy indeed.'

Her brown eyes are frank and clear.

'A better person than I might tell you that it was not important. That the money didn't make any difference. But it did, Claire. With all that money behind me, I felt absolutely safe in the world.'

'Where did Grace go?' you ask.

Evie frowns.

'I never knew. And I didn't ever try to find out. I simply couldn't live with her any longer, and she had to leave.'

'Did you miss her?'

Evie locks her eyes on yours.

'Claire, there isn't a single day, still, that I don't feel the loss of her.'

She holds your gaze, her eyes unguarded.

'I will miss her for the rest of my life.'

You shut Evie's bedroom door behind you quietly, still feeling her sadness. Light angles in through the window over the stairwell, creating distorted squares of sun on the floor in front of you. It occurs to you: this is the same door that Grace opened, all those years ago. This is where Grace stood, listening to Harold dying. See:

> *His awkward body on the landing a floor above you, the side of his head cradled by thick carpet, the hard floor underneath.*

You take a few steps up towards the second floor, hesitate, step back down. The house is silent.

Outside, you are slow, reluctant to leave the house and move beyond the reality that has been told back into existence here. At the gate, you turn and look up. The terracotta brick shines in the afternoon sun. The little gargoyle smiles down at you from under the eaves.

You had looked up *gargoyle*. You turned the thin pages of the dictionary hoping there would be a line drawing, but the illustration on that page was a bulb of garlic, split open to show the cloves.

Gargoyle. Like gargle; like gurgle. From the French word for 'throat.' You learned that gargoyles are water spouts. The water spews through them, away from the building, to keep the bricks dry.

You squint against the sun, picking out the details of the

little creature hunched under the eaves. It is entirely possible to feel affection for something that is ugly. And the opposite is true, of course. You can be repulsed by something that is beautiful.

Like Grace.

I knew she was evil.

And now you know what she was capable of. Something so cold, so awful that Evie had to send her away.

A ripple of satisfaction spreads in your chest, warm and sweet; you shudder.

Grace is not here now.

I am.

You turn away, close the cold iron gate behind you.

—

29

Evie talks about loving the sea.

'Even a calm sea is deceptive,' she says. 'It's quite remarkable, don't you think? How even a calm sea can be so dangerous just a short way from the shore.'

'And you like that about it?' you ask.

But she is not to be drawn into a discussion.

'The sea,' says Evie, 'Can't be caught. It can't be defined.'

Your mother loved the sea, too. You remember one hot day in her bedroom, the smell of cut grass spilling in through the open window. You were doing your homework, papers spread out on the floor. She was resting, eyes flickering under her eyelids, chest rising and falling to the hoarse sound of her breath. She opened her eyes, cleared her throat.

'I've just realized,' she said, 'That I will never swim in the sea again. Never even see it again. You should go to the sea for me, Claire.'

'I don't like the sea.'

'How can you not like the sea?' She laughed, then coughed.

You didn't try to explain. But even now, you avoid the sea. You don't like the glitter of light on the waves. The way you can't always tell where the sky ends and the sea begins. And the colours. The way they are neither one thing or the other – green, grey, blue – and in your cupped hands, no colour at all.

> There's a place like the sea in my mind. Like waves, churning.

> I stay away from it.

> The sea, the real sea outside, pulls me to that place in my mind; it makes me feel how unquiet I am.

You went on holiday once, somewhere by the sea, but cold. You stayed with your parents in a guesthouse where none of the bedding matched. There were sheets and blankets, not duvets. Patterned sheets, clean and fresh but faded, all the flowers in pastels.

The first morning, the woman who ran the place gave you porridge for breakfast. A wedge of porridge that looked like it had been cut with a cake knife. You made a well in the middle, filled it with cold milk, sprinkled brown sugar over it.

'This is better porridge, mum,' you said. 'You should make it like this.'

Your mother said nothing, looked at your father and then down at the tablecloth.

'Your mum's porridge is great,' he said. 'The best in the world.'

And your mother, still looking down, smiled to herself.

'Well I like it this way,' you said, and had porridge every morning for the whole week.

During the day, your parents sat in deckchairs while you explored the rock pools at low tide. You remember limpets and barnacles. Gritty sand. Your mother wore a silk scarf, burnt orange, the kind of colour that makes other women pale. It reflected in her eyes, on her skin and her glossed lips, making her brighter, even more vivid.

***

There is a little kitchen at the back of the nursery shop: a countertop with a sink, a kettle and some mugs, a fridge in the corner and a couple of wooden chairs. It has that not-quite-clean feeling that goes with shared kitchens.

Martin is leaning against the counter, looking through your photographs. He's taking his time, really looking. You pour cold water into the red mug for yourself, the white one for him. Your feel clumsy, your hands are trembling.

Be busy.

It doesn't matter if he doesn't like them.

You put the bottle of water back in the fridge, perch on one of the uncomfortable chairs. Your breathing isn't quite right; your lungs are full of air, and still you feel breathless. You sip the water; it feels wrong. The mug is thick, the water thin. You don't really want it, it's just something to do.

You turn your head so you don't have to watch Martin looking at your pictures; you stare out of the tiny window at the patch of field behind the shop. There are poppies along the edges. Orange-red, transitory. When the seed heads go brown and spill their tiny seeds, you will start counting the days shorter.

You can hear the sound of each photograph, thick and glossy, as Martin puts it back on the pile. You had been surprised how substantial they were when you went back to the camera shop and Joe, Manager had printed them out for you.

You wonder which one Martin is looking at now. Maybe the one of the edges of petals. Flawed, rough, irregular, the edges of white carnation petals. The carnations were in a bucket outside a shop on a busy corner in town. You knelt on the dirty pavement, the sound of traffic loud around you; you focused the camera and your mind on the serrated flowers. You got so close they were unrecognizable, they looked like curling paper or strange white fabric.

You had gone into town that day to take photos of sharp edges, hard surfaces, plastic and glass. But you found it difficult. You kept seeking out natural things. The carnations in the bucket. The drops of water on the rim of the bucket. A dandelion springing up between paving slabs; tough pink valerian clinging to a wall.

You took a few images of manmade things. The curve of a concrete wall. Old ironwork railings painted black as thick as liquorice. Mortar between old bricks, close enough to see the individual grains of sand in the mix. But the textures did not draw you in. Not like the fruit and flowers at the grocery store.

Luminous red strawberry flesh, dimpled; each dimple inhabited by a little seed, sharp and purposeful.

Grapes. Translucent, so you could see the shadow of the seeds inside.

The feathery anthers of a lily, the stigma overtly sexual, puckered and glistening.

You take another sip of water from the mug, then get up and move closer to the window. The windowsill is dusty, smells slightly damp. Your breathing is still uncomfortable so you take a deliberately deep breath and puff against the glass. You draw lines in the mist with your fingertip, squint through them at the poppies.

In town, a man had joked with you, offered to pose for you.

'But it would break your camera, hey, love?'

You were relieved when he moved away, laughing. You don't take pictures of people. You don't want the relationship, even with the barrier of the camera lens between you.

The kitchen is quiet. You realize that Martin has finished looking at the photographs. You stare firmly out the window.

It doesn't matter if he doesn't like them.

Martin says: 'These are really good, Claire.'

And warmth settles around your shoulders like a light blanket. You turn, check the planes of his face for anything that seems insincere. But he is purely enthusiastic.

'You really have a talent,' he says. 'You make things seem

different. They look unfamiliar, so close. More interesting.'

He picks up the photo on top of the pile, studies it again, then shows it to you.

It is a damselfly's wing. The struts in the wing are like wires, mechanical, irregularly spaced, supporting the shiny transparent film of the wing material.

'See?'

He puts it down again and nods at you, clearly pleased.

You can feel your mouth pulling itself into a smile.

'It's how I like to look at things,' you say.

—

Her eyes are shut but you know she is not asleep. You touch the soft bedspread with your fingertips.

'It's started getting colder,' you say. 'I had to wear a cardigan today.'

No response. Evie is not interested in the shifting of the season. It has always fascinated you, nature's steady slipping from one state into another, its readiness to change. You are on the lookout, always, for the signs.

Today, the yellow roses around Evie's door are completely finished, the petals shrivelled and brown. It doesn't seem very long ago, after the first flush of roses, that you brought your secateurs in with you to deadhead them. It was hot that day. Margaret provided a stepladder and you stood on the top rung, reaching up for the crisp flower shells, feeling sweat gather at your hairline. The secateurs sliced through the dark green stems twelve inches down from the old blooms to encourage a second flush of flowers. Margaret gave you lemonade – the shop-bought kind with bubbles, not the freshly squeezed lemon juice that Evie drinks. It was strange to be outside Evie's house, busy up and down the stepladder, sweating, knowing she was inside, in the cool bedroom upstairs, absolutely still. There were enough of the scratchy flower heads to fill three plastic carrier bags. You gave them to Margaret to dispose of.

You find it hard to look at Margaret these days. You want to be able to see her with compassion – but when she's in front of you it's as hard as ever to get beyond the sullen lumpiness of her. What must it be like for Evie, knowing that her own child is so completely unattractive? Evie, who appreciates beautiful things, sparkling people.

Now the second flush of roses has been and gone. But this time the dead flowers will remain on their stems and turn into shiny red rosehips. The fruit of the rose, they will glow amongst the dull branches as the days darken.

You hear Evie's breathing change, realize her eyes are open, that she is looking at you.

'Tomorrow, I have something to say,' she announces. 'And something to ask. Something important.'

'Can't you say it now?'

'No, no, not now,' says Evie. 'Tomorrow.' She turns her head away. You are dismissed.

The mirror is relentless. You are wrapped in a black cape, head offered up, wet hair hanging around your pale face. You have nowhere else to look. The young man with the scissors stands behind you, puts his hands on your shoulders, talks to your reflection. His fingernails are broad and shiny, but the rest of him is narrow; tall and slim. He has a long face, a long nose. His name, he says, is Aaron. He wants to know what you have in mind.

'Just a trim,' you say.

'Perhaps some layers to give it more body, more shape?' He ruffles your hair up with his fingers, demonstrates more body, more shape. His own hair is bleached nearly white, arranged in careful spikes.

'Would I still be able to tie it back for work?'

'Oh yes, definitely.'

'Then that would be fine.'

'Excellent,' he says.

He pulls up a stool on wheels, starts at the back. Comb, grip, snip. You stare at the mirror, catch the reflected eye of the woman on the opposite side of the room. Like you, she is trussed up in a black cape, her hair is in silver foil. She looks away. Perhaps there is an etiquette here that you are unaware of. Perhaps it is not the done thing, to look at other people while they are half-done, in the process of creating themselves. You look back at your own face, shut your eyes.

'When did you last have it cut?'

His voice is quiet. He is mindful of being in your personal space, next to your ear. You open your eyes, speak to his reflection.

'Um. I can't remember. I cut it myself, usually.'

'Okay. That would explain it.' He smiles briefly, then looks down again, gets on with the job. You shut your eyes again.

The stroking of the comb is soothing. The busy salon is full of sound, a cushion of sound that folds around you, the hum of voices, the steady beat of music. The air is perfumed, sweet with just a hint of the bite of peroxide.

Evie has something to tell me.

That she has included you in her Will, perhaps? She has hinted. And Margaret Keyes seems to think so.

The thought of being Evie's beneficiary makes something flutter in your stomach. It's not the money. It's the idea you could be that important to her. To Evie, who is special, and not easy, who is reticent with her affection.

There is gentle pressure on the top of your head, you tilt it down, feel the scissors whispering at the nape of your neck.

And she has something to ask.

Perhaps she wants you to visit more often. She might ask you to stay overnight. Maybe even on a regular basis. You could have your own room.

You become aware that the combing and cutting has stopped. Aaron breaks orbit from around your chair; you can feel the absence of him. Then he's back. You open your eyes; he has a jar of something to show you.

'This is a great product,' he says. 'You only need a bit and it lasts forever.'

He rubs some into the palm of his hands, then into your hair.

'I'll just blow this dry for you,' he says.

You watch in the mirror as, under his quick hands, your hair dries thicker, shinier. When he is finished, you ask: 'Will I be able to do this at home?'

'Easy peasy,' he says. 'The layers do all the work.'

You buy a small jar of the styling product, leave a tip.

———

30

Does she seem any different today? Is she excited? It's hard to tell with Evie. You sit at the end of the bed, she fixes her eyes on you. Yes, she's excited.

'Claire. You are wearing your hair differently today,' she says, twinkling.

'Yes,' you touch your neck. 'I had it cut.'

'It's lovely, my dear.'

'Thank you.'

You notice your breathing is too shallow, take a deep breath to catch up, hope you are not obviously nervous. The clock ticks like a snare drum in the silence.

'Of course, you are wondering what I want to say,' says Evie at last. She is smiling, head cocked slightly to one side.

'So I won't keep you in suspense, my dear. It is simply this. First, that you have become very special to me – '

You feel the blood climb up from your collarbone, heating your neck; you have to look away.

' – indeed, Claire, I never imagined that there was room in me to feel a connection with another human being, not after all the things... Well you know, my dear, I have told you of them. And it is through that telling, perhaps, that I have come to trust you to such a degree. I do trust you, Claire, to listen fairly and to be slow to judge. And I trust your sense of what is fair and right.'

She pauses, turns her head to the drinking straw beside her and takes a sip of lemonade, then continues.

'And so I am going to ask you to help me in what has become my heart's desire. I'm hoping you will want to help me.'

The pause is like a question, so you answer yes – but it sounds like a growl because your throat is so full.

You cough and speak again, 'Yes, of course, Evie. I'll do anything I can to help.'

'Will you, Claire? We shall see. Because what I'm going to request of you requires you to be very unselfish – perhaps more selfless than you are able.'

She is silent then, waiting perhaps, for you to raise your eyes. So you do, and you have never seen Evie look more beautiful. She is soft and shining and very serious. You could rest forever in the light of her eyes.

'It's simply this, darling girl,' she says.

'Claire, will you help me die?'

———

31

In bed, sitting with your back against the wall, looking into the dark.

You are thinking that there are different kinds of panic, but only the one word to describe them all, and it's not enough. It's clearly not enough, because people say they're having a panic attack these days, even when it's obviously not a panic attack, which would leave them ripped open; shredded in ways they can't even imagine.

There should be as many different words as there are different kinds of panic. And more than anything, there should be a word for the kind of panic that hangs like a bat beneath your breastbone, wrapped in naked skin wings, shrieking on a level that no-one else can hear.

You slide down, turn on your side, bunch the duvet up against your back so it feels like you are being held. You cannot close your eyes. When you close your eyes, you see Evie's face, hear her words. You roll over on your back again, stare up at the dark ceiling.

You remember this feeling.

You went in to your mother to give her a pink tablet and her warm milk, and she smiled. You loved her for smiling when you knew she was hurting, but you hated the smile. It was a thin smile, pulled tight over teeth that seemed too large for her mouth. It stretched the skin of her face.

The tablets were shiny, easy to swallow. She took one with water. Then you helped her drink the milk, your hand hovering under the cup in case she lost hold of it. While she drank, you followed the stripes on the bedspread with your eyes.

As a little girl, you had imagined the stripes were a map. You would sit on your parent's double bed surrounded by familiar countryside. The herringbone stripe was a railway track, the yellow one a road. And then there was a river (blue) and a green line of hills, another railway, and so on. But now your mother was surrounded by the map, and now it was a foreign country, hers alone, and dangerous. Your father was sleeping on the settee in the living room.

'My sweet girl,' she said to you, when she had finished the milk.

'I'll leave some water here, shall I, Mum? In case you need some in the night?'

You reached out for the bottle of tablets, to put them back up on the shelf. Her hand stopped you. Very dry and thin, it rested on yours, light as ashes.

'Leave that,' she said. 'Give your mum a kiss.'

You had stopped kissing her weeks ago. You couldn't bear how the taste of her skin had changed from the powdery freshness you grew up with. How the feel of it had changed, become something else, unfamiliar and frightening. You thought she understood this. She never said anything, never asked. Until that night, and you couldn't say no. You brushed her skin with your lips, trying not to breathe in the smell of vinegar.

'Night, Mum,' you mumbled, and fled.

Even after the funeral, your father never mentioned it. You had been sure there would be repercussions, even wondered if you could go to prison.

Months passed; still your father said nothing. You waited for his anger to spill over but he never confronted you. And he never tried to ease your mind. He could have told you it was too much responsibility for a sixteen year old. That even a grown-up could have forgotten, that one time.

Except, of course, you hadn't forgotten. And you had gone to bed as usual, even though part of you had been shouting inside your head: *You can't just go to bed. You have to tell Dad. You have to get up and tell Dad. Why don't you get up and tell Dad?* while you lay there, tears sliding past your ears into your pillow.

The floor is hard on your knees. There is something in the act of kneeling, something that says *please* before you even open your mind or your mouth to ask for help. But you are frozen there, you don't get any further, you know it won't work. No-one is listening. Not to you, not to anyone, not in that way.

You bury your face in the duvet, inhale the smell of the bedding, the smell that your own body has left there. You stand up, rub the creases out of your knees, get back into bed.

—

32

Marching, eyes on the ground, chanting under your breath.
Earth.
Stone.
Leaf.
Root.
Earth.
Twig.
Stone.

The path unfolds in shades of brown. Your old boots measure it out in noisy footsteps, crushing dry leaves and twigs, sounding the compacted earth like a drum. You breathe in with an open mouth, seek out the smell of things undisturbed, of quiet decay, feel the taste of the woods on your teeth and tongue. You want your senses to overpower your thoughts. You want to stop the words in your head.

'I lie here,' she said. *'Replaying memories. I don't want to, but they force themselves on me and I have so little with which to distract myself. I listen to the radio and a song or a sentence, even a tone of voice, has the power to throw me back into the past. And it's more real than the world I inhabit now.'*

Around you, the smooth grey trunks of ash saplings rise up like wands, the space between them luminous. The sky is irrelevant here. There are stripes of pale and dark, the occasional slice of sunlight across the path, the green of the moss shining in the shadows.

'During the day, my dreams feel too close. They crowd around me, even when I am awake.'

The path narrows, gets spongier and less even. The smell of leaf mould is stronger. The untrodden floor of the woods spreads out around you, a random pattern of fallen branches, stems, ivy, twigs. You walk through a cloud of midges, brush them away from your face.

'I get caught in a loop, replaying the same scene in my mind over and over. And I get scared, Claire. So much of what is in my mind is frightening. Remember what it was like to be a child – to be certain there was something in the room with you, something formless and malevolent? As adults we learn to protect ourselves from those fears, we build fences against them. My fences are dissolving. Often now, fear spills out of me, fills the room. And it will get worse.'

You stop. Without the sound of your footfalls there is only your breathing. You are overwhelmed by the stillness around you, the silent uprising of the trees. The sense of being alone settles around you like a snowfall. With no eyes upon you, nothing to respond to, you feel your face slacken.

'I know what is happening to me,' she said. 'And I want to put a stop to it. I want to be the one who decides. I will not be one of those vacant dears who can't remember. Who have nothing left of themselves and are utterly dependant. You think I am dependant lying here? My dear, you have no idea how much freedom I have now – to form my own opinions, to decide how I interact with others, to choose my thoughts, to learn, to listen, to understand. As long as I am in possession of my own mind.'

You were on the other side of the room, by the window, the cold wood of the sill pressing into the small of your back. You couldn't quite get your breath, even though your lungs felt full of air. You had to breathe out and breathe back in again.

'But I haven't noticed,' you bleated, finally. 'I've seen nothing…'

'You can't think I am imagining this, my dear? There are test results. I'm told that the first signs aren't obvious to others. You wouldn't see it yet. It will get worse.'

'You could wait…'

She said nothing.

'You could wait until it gets worse…'

She raised her eyebrows, ever so slightly. Your throat was closing, the base of your tongue felt swollen and metallic.

How can she ask me this?

'Poor Claire. Don't think, my dear, that I ask this lightly. I know what you must be thinking. See, you are moving away from me even now, gathering yourself inwards, creating distance between us. But don't do that, Claire. Wait until you hear what I have to say.'

You swallowed. Breathed. She nodded and smiled.

'Claire. I know what great harm your mother did you. She made use of you. She gave you no choice. I am not doing that, my dear. I am not tricking you, manipulating you. I am asking – honestly. Directly. And whatever you decide, my dear, I will respect your decision.'

I don't have to do it, then.

I just have to think about it.

I can think about it and then say no.

'Listen, Claire. We all try to recreate our pasts. We replay the old relationships and situations over and over, hoping that we will be able to mend them, to make them right. We want to heal ourselves. And mostly we do that without being aware of it.' You had never seen her so intense, her eyes so full of compassion they were almost liquid.

'Look, my dear. You have the chance to mend something here. This time, you can choose. It would be a kindness to me,

Claire. An astonishing gift. But only if it is your choice.'

A sudden flurry of feathers stirs the air above the forest canopy. A flock of birds rises and wheels away in a tumble of sound and thrashing air. Somewhere to your left, a lone bird responds with a muted whistle. You start moving again. Slowly.

'And I promise you, Claire, I would never, never ask this of you if I didn't truly believe, in my deepest heart, that it might be a healing for you as well as a release for me. Dear child, you must know I couldn't hurt you.'

Earth.

Stone.

Leaf.

Twig.

A rook coughs in one of the tall trees. You look up. Within the mix of greens in the canopy above you, half the leaves are turning yellow. You head left at the fork in the path, past a fallen tree trunk. In the leaf mould beneath, there are flaky white toadstools with lids like bells.

Another hundred yards and you're there. And as always, you don't realise it at first. From this side, the Witch Tree gradually dissolves out of the woods. Greengrey bark. Impossible branches. Roots like complicated knotwork. From the other side, you can see the whole of the massive tree in its own clearing. But if James hadn't told you, you would never have known it was here.

'It takes seven people to get their arms around the trunk. Must be the best part of five hundred years old,' he'd said, loading hedging into the back of his truck. You should come and see it.'

'Is it named after a real witch?'

He ran one hand through his grey hair, making it stick out at angles. He smelled of new sawdust and Nag Champa incense.

'Mary Chailey. She was hanged there.' He shook his head. 'I know more than one person who believes she's still there, in spirit.'

'What do you think?'

He rubbed one hand over the grey stubble on his chin.

'The poor girl was hanged, but I doubt she was a witch. It's the tree itself that's the witch. And if the girl is still around, it's because the tree is healing her.'

There is a place against the trunk, between two massive roots. You put your blanket on the ground there, not flat like a picnic blanket, rumpled like a nest. You can sit there, between the two roots, with your back against the ancient trunk, and feel held by the living wood.

Gradually, your heartbeat slows, becomes quiet. You tune into the rustling of things. The cracking of twigs, the whisper of air through the leaves. You rest the back of your head against the trunk and look up at the architecture of the grey branches above you. They spread over and around you; a living dome, the bottom branches hang low enough to touch the ground at the outside edge.

Evie wants to die.

Something cracks in your chest and you feel the heat of tears on your face. You wipe your face on your sleeve. You don't want to cry. You want to think clearly.

There have been times when even your breathing was in time with hers, your chest rising and falling in concert with the soft movement of her covers. There have been times when you have felt her touch you with her eyes, literally felt it. How are you going to be able to let her go?

'Please. Evie. No.'

Without meaning to, you have spoken aloud. And then you feel embarrassed even though there is no one around for miles; you look around to check.

A pale girl is sitting in one of the low sweeping branches, her bare feet dangling just a few inches above the ground. She's watching you the way an animal watches, without self-consciousness.

'Mary Chailey?'

She can't be more than fourteen or fifteen years old. In a coarse grey smock, her thin red hair cut painfully close to the scalp, she looks like a child. You can't imagine what she has been through, can't bear to think of it. But she doesn't appear distressed now. You wipe your eyes and try again.

'Hello, Mary.'

She smiles.

'Mary,' you say, wanting to offer something to help her mending. 'I am so sorry for what happened to you. I really am sorry. Those people who did that to you, they were very ignorant and wrong.'

She smiles at you again, then hops off the branch and walks towards you. Almost close enough to touch, she steps past you into the greygreen trunk of the tree, disappears in it.

You unzip your rucksack, take out your cold drink and a cream envelope, one of your mother's letters. You chose it before you came out, let your fingers hover, felt the prickle over the right one, tucked it into your rucksack without looking at it.

> If ever you had anything useful to say to me, Mum, let it be now.

You uncap the drink and take a long swallow, open the envelope. There's only one page.

Dearest Claire,

I wish I had found the right words when I had all the time in the world. Now there is not much time and I'm still not sure I can find them.

I have been wondering if perhaps I was not as good a mother to you as I thought I was. I believed I made sacrifices for you. Now I am not sure.

The truth is, I think some women are not meant to be mothers. It is not in their nature.

I have learned something though. That there are consequences for what we choose. Sooner or later, we have to look at our choices and see how they have conspired to make us into who we are. I don't know if there is a way to live that doesn't involve regret. There will always be the things we didn't do.

All my love.

You lean back against the tree and close your eyes.

Your mother would be on Evie's side in this, you think. *By all means, get Claire to help you die. She's good at that. Has past experience, you know.*

No. I don't really believe that.

You sit up and take the dictionary out of your rucksack. You run the tip of your finger down the edges of the closed white pages. Solid and soft; it is like stroking the surface of a river.

There is something about me that is easily used. It doesn't matter how I will feel, how I will be left.

You let the dictionary fall open, close your eyes and allow your fingertip to fall onto a word.

Friable: Easily crumbled.

You almost laugh.

Then you look up *choice:* Decide between possibilities.

And *choose:* Decide to do one thing rather than another.

Then you look inside the front cover. *For Claire, from Dad xxx.*

It's getting cooler. The shadows seem deeper now, the air heavier. You're tired. Not sleepy, but tired in the way you feel after a day spent moving heavy bags of compost. Tired to the bone.

'It would be a kindness to me, Claire. An astonishing gift. But only if it is your choice.'

It doesn't feel like a gift to you. It feels like a loss that will leave you reeling, derailed. If you could wait until Evie was clearly in distress, it might be easier. You see:

Evie in her bed, eyes staring, terrified. Her head swings from side to side, but she can't reach the buzzer. Margaret has moved the buzzer away because Evie presses it too often, every time she panics about where she is, every time she gets scared. You see tears in Evie's eyes, and confusion.

'Are you sure you can't wait any longer?' you had asked.

'We need to do it soon, while I am still myself, so you can be certain it was my wish. So you never have to wonder whether I really meant it.'

Once, at the nursery, you found a mouse that had been mauled by a cat and left for dead. Only it wasn't dead. There was blood in its nose and eyes, one paw was gone. But it was still breathing, its small body shuddering. It would have been easier to lay it aside in the long grass, let it die unseen, slowly. You placed the edge of your spade against its neck and trod down hard. You had to grit your teeth. But it was clearly, undeniably, the kindest thing.

You tip your head back and look into the tree above you. There are yellows amongst the green here too. You wonder what it will be like in the winter, this tree, bare of leaves, its wood naked. In winter, the colours of wood are easier to appreciate. Grey browns, green browns, green greys, silver greys. It is a muted palette of colours but one that moves you. It is always in the winter that you wish you were an artist. Perhaps this winter you will take photographs, not just of the close-up wood, but of the sweep of naked trees on the hills. The highlights of yellow willow, silver birch. The branches and trunks, from a distance, like brush strokes.

She has no-one else to ask.

You tip your head down again, rest your forehead on your knees.

Your mother chose. When she could no longer endure it, when each breath was a labour, when she was separated already, from the people she loved, by a wall of pain. She chose.

You realise that in spite of everything, in spite of the way your mother used you, you believe she had the right to choose.

And so does Evie.

33

The countryside swings by, a mix of green and gold. Even the air is bright today, the glowing bright that happens in early autumn. The old power station chimney is clean and silver against the sky. You begin to gather yourself in readiness for your stop. It's a mental thing – pull your bag an inch closer, rock your feet on the floor in anticipation. Other passengers are doing the same. No-one is standing yet, but small movements rustle through the carriage. Your stomach lurches; this part of the journey is over, you are closer to Evie and to giving her your answer.

You picture her face. Calm. Reserved.

'You have an answer for me Claire?' Her voice like agate, smooth.

And you imagine telling her.

'Yes Evie, I will help you. If that's what you need. Even though I don't know how I will bear to lose you.'

You see Evie's face then, how it softens, becomes warmer. Her eyes fill.

'Claire,' she says. 'My dear. Thank you so very much.'

The train slows, moves forward into the station. You feel queasy.

This requires a different kind of courage. Not just feeling afraid and doing it anyway; being willing to risk doing the wrong thing. You lean back against the headrest, the curve of upholstered foam presses the base of your skull.

Eyes closed, you look for a calm place within yourself, the place that is at peace with your decision. But there is no peace. Even your breathing is an irritant, a shallow rush that disturbs your chest, leaves your solar plexus feeling bothered. You try taking deeper breaths, they agitate deeper.

Maybe she will have changed her mind today.

You smile at that, the idea of Evie changing her mind about anything. You look out the window, see only the extraordinary old woman who is waiting for you.

Imagine:

Being unable to move at all. Searching other people's eyes; hardly daring to hope that someone might notice what you need, that someone might be willing to let it matter to them.

People can be so polite; seemingly concerned but completely unreachable.

I am going to say yes.

But you have three conditions.

It has to be something painless – you need to know she will feel nothing.

You will leave straight away. Do what needs to be done and then turn and walk out of the room. You will not stay with her, will not watch her die.

And finally, whatever means you use, Evie's death must appear natural or accidental. Any chance there could be public scrutiny or legal consequences would make it impossible. You don't have that much courage.

The train has come to a stop. As you stand up, the door between carriages slides open and the tattooed man steps into the aisle. You have never seen him out of his seat – he is shorter than you would have guessed. He scans the length of the carriage, sees you and nods, takes the nearest empty seat.

He watches as you move away from him towards the exit door. You have to move, there are people behind you in the aisle. You twist round before you step off the train, crane your neck. He is still watching. On the platform, you are standing only a couple of feet away from his window. The tattooed man holds your gaze through the thick glass as the train begins to move off.

You watch as it disappears down the curve of the tracks, then make your way to the turnstiles.

———

You are walking on a carpet of yellow leaves, under trees that were planted a hundred years ago. They are horse chestnuts, not sweet chestnuts for roasting. The spiky brown seedpods hang in pairs amongst the branches; soon they will split open, reveal shining redbrown hearts that will spill out onto the wide avenue.

Your palms are damp. Already, you are feeling anxious about the details, about how the thing will be carried out. But there's no need to worry about that; Evie will have a plan, or she'll come up with one. All she needs to know now is that you are willing.

The pavement is gritty under your feet; the air smells of ivy and damp brick – and of autumn. You think how strange it is, that everyone recognises the smell of autumn, even if they can't describe it. It is a relic of our animal selves, the ability to smell the change of season. You think about a dog's nose, black and rubbery, and picture a tiny black rubbery replica tucked away in the part of your brain where the animal instincts reside.

From the corner of your eye, you notice a man on the pavement to your right, half hidden by the hedge. He is standing, waiting. You step away from him, glance sideways as you pass. Then you stop. It's Edward from the windmill. Edward, who is never anywhere but at the windmill, dying over and over again.

Now he's here, red jacket bright against the green shadows of the hedge, staring at his feet.

'Edward?' He doesn't look up, he's already starting to fade.

'Edward, wait! What are you doing here?' But he's gone, leaving you unsettled. Edward's world is in the clearing in the woods, in the gently rotting windmill. He shouldn't be here on the hard pavement. Like the tattooed man in the wrong carriage on the train, he's out of place.

There's a sudden clatter of wings in the branches above you. You look up in time to see the grey shape of a pigeon break through the leaves into the sky and circle over to a lamp post on the opposite side of the avenue.

A few steps further and Mary Chailey is in front of you, alongside the little girl from Evie's garden. They stand together, blocking your path. The little girl is still damp, hair halfwet halfdry, hanging in ribbons. You can see pale flesh through the thin wet fabric of her dress. She is staring at you the way children stare, the way that you stare when you know you're looking at a ghost – with no concern for how your gaze will be received. Her eyes are grey. You haven't seen the colour of her eyes before, only the fan of her hair as she sinks under the water.

Next to her, shorn, out of context, Mary appears mad, derelict. Even more so because she is speaking forcefully, her face intense with feeling. She might even be shouting. But you can't hear a word. The sound doesn't carry from where she is to where you are.

'Excuse me.'

You flinch at the sound of the voice behind you, realize you are in the way, standing stock still in the middle of the pavement.

'Sorry.' You move aside to let the woman pass, watching as she pushes the pram into Mary's thin body. Through Mary's body. You expect Mary to disappear but she stays where she is, still trying to communicate.

'I'm sorry Mary, I can't hear you.' You shake your head.

Then you realize how strange you look standing here talking aloud to no-one.

It doesn't matter what I look like.

This is important. It must be important or they wouldn't be here.

You strain towards Mary, trying to catch any vibration of sound. Her lips move urgently. You hear nothing. You shake your head. She falls still. Sighs. The little wet girl sighs too. They fade.

You are left alone feeling dizzy, slightly sick. You want to sit down but there is nowhere and Evie's house is only another block away. Taking deep breaths, you put one foot in front of the other, ignoring the buzzing in your ears, focusing on the feel of cool air against your clammy skin.

It must be about Evie.

Maybe they know how scared I am and they want to help.

Stop. Breathe. Start again. One foot at a time. You count your steps in sets of four. By the time you reach Evie's gate, your heart has stopped racing and you are breathing normally. But you feel slightly unreal, as though something has shifted – either you or everything else – moved slightly out of alignment so that you aren't quite connected.

You use your key, hope Margaret isn't around. You don't want to see Margaret today. The door opens onto an empty hallway. Almost empty. Wrapped in the smell of beeswax and motes of dust, there is something else here. It writhes down the stairs, down from the attic, rubbing itself against the banisters, eager for you. It welcomes you in, carries you up the stairs on an excited current, pushes you against Evie's bedroom door, so you knock and almost stumble into the room. Then it falls away from you suddenly like a wind dropping, leaving everything silent.

There is Evie, her eyes intense above a wry smile of welcome.

Beyond her, sitting in the chair on the other side of the bed, knitting without looking at her needles, there is Nanny Bee.

'Nanny Bee –' the words don't reach your throat. Your chest opens, your rib cage expands, releases its grip on your heart. Nanny Bee is here. But she doesn't look at you, she is looking at Evie. So you do too. You wonder for a moment whether Evie can see Nanny Bee, but she can't.

'Hello, Claire.' Evie speaks softly, seriously.

You move towards her, stop at the foot of the bed.

'You're pale,' she says. 'I'm so sorry, my dear; it hurts me to see you looking so tense.' Her eyes are warm and liquid, full of care, full of understanding.

'I could never have put you through this, Claire, if I didn't believe that in the long run, it will bring you peace. I know you'll make the right choice.'

Standing at the foot of her bed, you want nothing more than to live up to Evie's belief in you. You can see how small she is, how incredibly slight. Her skin is almost translucent, the cheekbones seem to glow through her skin.

'What have you decided, my dear?'

And that's when Nanny Bee stands up, puts her knitting into her apron pocket, and moves around the bed towards you. You feel a surge of affection; after all this time, her face is still absolutely familiar to you. The mild eyes, tucked into their folds of soft wrinkly skin, the big pores on her nose, the rough red of her cheeks. She stands in front of you, closer than she has ever been before, so that you cannot see around her. Nanny Bee's eyes hold yours, and it feels like that, like being held. Then she raises one hand, palm flat, and places it on the flat of your chest, just under your collarbone, above your heart. The other she rests on your shoulder. You can't feel her. Not physically. There is no weight, no warmth, and yet you know that Nanny Bee is holding you with all the strength in her ghostly body. She moves her face even closer. And slowly, not taking her eyes off yours, she shakes her head.

Her meaning couldn't be clearer. *No*.

And you feel immediately lighter. Like the weight of the world has been lifted from you. A silent sob of gratitude catches in your throat.

Nanny Bee disappears then. You watch her fade, but you don't feel her go. For all you know, she could still be holding you, still have her hand pressed above your heart.

'Claire?' Evie is watching you with narrow eyes, waiting for an answer. You take a breath.

'I'm sorry, Evie.'

Her expression doesn't change. She waits for more.

'I'm so sorry. I thought I could do it. I wanted so much to be able to. Because I do believe you have the right to choose – even though it would hurt me so much to lose you.'

You sit at the end of the bed, back against the footboard. It's hard to look at her now. You don't want to see anger in Evie's face. You don't want to cause her pain. You look down at the bedspread; the pattern of blue and purple is blurred.

'You asked me to think seriously about it and do what I think is right. I've thought about nothing else all week.' Your voice trails off. You breathe and start again.

'I know you think it would be a good thing for me. But I know it won't.' Your voice steadies. 'Even though I love you. Even though I want, more than anything, to help you. It would hurt me to do this.'

You look up again. She is listening intently; you still have no idea what she is thinking, feeling.

'I'm sorry, Evie, I just can't. It's too much for me to carry. It was too much for me as a child, and it's too much now. I have to say no.'

Evie's face is calm. Perhaps her lips have tightened a little.

'No?' She tilts her head, listening to the echo of your answer in the quiet room. Then she smiles.

'Of course, Claire. You have to say no.'

And then Evie says:

'You've never done anything requiring courage in the whole of your life, have you, my dear?' And her voice has never sounded like this before, polished and smooth, but harder. Like flint. Like a sharp stone weapon.

'But this is no more than I expected, really; you were such a ninny about Margaret being my daughter. How difficult was it to come to this decision of yours, Claire? Did you even make one or are you just doing what is easiest?'

'Evie.'

Her name comes out of your throat several notes higher than usual, sounds almost like a whine. She doesn't blink. You lift your hands in front of you as if it might be possible to pat down her hostility. It is not.

'What a shame, Claire. You're no better than that lump of a woman. There is nothing extraordinary in either of you.'

You feel your throat closing.

'But you said –'

You swallow, force more words out.

'You said I had a choice. I'm sorry. I know you wanted this very badly.'

'Wanted what? To die?' She laughs, and it is a lovely, light sound.

'Of course I don't want to die! I am too vital, too rich within myself. That you could believe I was losing my senses!'

She looks you in the eye.

'I'm not ill, you stupid girl. I am just *bored*. Bored silly lying here, away from the world, unable to reach anyone who matters. It has relieved my boredom somewhat, playing this game with you. It had become tedious, with only Margaret to play with.'

Her eyes still fixed on yours, she shakes her head.

'And so I have endured your dreary company for these months. Your long face and your sad history.'

The room seems to tilt. You grasp for something solid, steady your voice.

'You don't mean that, Evie. You said –' you try to remember her exact words – 'You said it meant the world to you to tell me your story.'

'My dear, you flatter yourself. Although the game has been interesting. I had no idea, when I asked for someone to visit me, that it would work out so well. With your background, your previous experience. You were perfect, really.'

She smiles, looks genuinely pleased.

'It's been fascinating.'

The clock is louder than ever, slower than ever, beating the heavy seconds. Listening to it, your own energy bleeds away; your entire body sags. It's an effort just to sit upright.

'And what would you have done if I had said yes?' You hear the weariness in your own voice.

Evie ponders.

'Mm. I don't know my dear. You have disappointed me and now we shall never know.'

You stand up, unsteady.

'No, don't go yet,' she says almost casually. 'Tell me more, Claire, about what you feel now. I am truly interested in how you are making sense of all this. In spite of the fact that you have had the temerity to refuse me.'

For a moment, the mask slips. She looks hungry, needy. As though your feelings could feed some part of her that is starving.

> She doesn't want me to go because that will be the end of it.

> The game will be over.

You move towards the door. It's hard to put one foot in front of the other. The floor is covered in a thick grey mist that churns above the carpets, sucks at your ankles. There are whispers.

'*Stay. Do it.*

Not out of love. Out of anger.

Do it because she is hurting you.'

Raising your hand to the doorknob, you glance back at Evie. She is shining, holding you with her gaze, willing you to stay.

And now you can see that the light in her eyes is something other than love.

You close the door quietly, firmly, behind you and walk slowly down the staircase without touching the balustrade. Margaret comes through the kitchen door, wiping her hands on her apron, looks up and sees you on the landing, waits for you at the bottom of the stairs. As bland as lard, she casts her deep eyes over your face. Her eyebrows lift slightly as she notices something is wrong. Poor Margaret. Stupid, ignorant Margaret.

'That woman,' you say, as you pass her, indicating upstairs with a tilt of your head, 'Is your mother.'

34

You have worked your way through the alphabet, cutting out the dead and dying stems, putting anything that looks diseased into a plastic trug, the rest into the wheelbarrow. Now amongst the V's, you are cutting back the tall dry verbascum stems that were once spires of watercolour flowers, oranges and pinks. It is an effort. Your arms and feet are leaden; you can feel the overcast sky pressing on you. You check the pots of evergreen vinca, cut out a few straggling stems. Then you balance the trug on top of the wheelbarrow, heft the cold metal handles and wheel the barrow across the uneven carpark.

Behind the storage sheds, the galvanised steel burner is still smoking, the embers at the bottom still alive. You add crumpled sheets of newspaper, watch as the paper catches alight. When there's a good new flame, you feed in the contents of the trug, the stems and leaves that are blemished with rust, mildew, leaf spot. The thick gloves mean you can work without fear of scratches or burns, but you have no dexterity. When you pull them off, your palms and fingers are damp.

You stand back and watch the seeping smoke, the glow of the embers at the ventilation holes around the bottom. Your chest hurts physically; your heart is swollen, tender tissue bruising itself against your ribs.

I never imagined that there was room in me to feel a

connection with another human being.

She said that.

When you are older, it will make your heart ache that you didn't know how lovely you were.

She said that.

And: *I trust you, Claire, to listen fairly and to be slow to judge.*

Of course, Evie is an expert, has been deceiving people for a long time. She even told you how. You remember all too well the pleasure she took in her seven rules:

Show them you understand.

Be entranced by them.

Tell them secrets.

Praise them.

Repeat what they tell you.

Be silent sometimes.

Maintain the semblance of equality.

Shame rises in you like a tide.

I made it so easy for her.

You poke the burner with a long stick, imagine the diseased leaves and stems burning away, leaving papery white ashes and nothing else.

You have replayed that last scene with Evie in your mind a hundred times. In your imagination, you turn and say something as you leave the room. Something devastating; something that makes her regret what she has done. But even now, you don't know what that would be.

Footsteps. Mr Holub is on his way back to the main house; he makes a detour to come and stand by you and you watch the burner together. He is wearing a red-checked padded jacket, like a lumberjack. He looks small within it.

'It is good, the smell, hey?' He inhales loudly to demonstrate how good, the smell of bonfire smoke on cold air. You nod weakly, say nothing. Mr Holub pats his chest with one knotted hand, the knuckles look swollen and painful. He smiles, moves off towards the house.

You leave the burner sulking smoke, wheel the barrow a bit further along to the big wooden compost bins. Two of the bins are full and covered with pieces of old carpet. You stop at the third and fork in the contents of the barrow. The muscles of your solar plexus are knotted, your chest rigid. You throw the last of the clippings into the bin with more force than is necessary.

Finished, you lean the barrow against the compost bin. And still you don't want to face anyone. So instead of going back to the shop, which is where you are supposed to be, you busy yourself scraping moss off the surface of the soil in the potted shrubs. You spend an hour kneeling in the gravel, until your knees are damp and sore, your feet cold in your boots, your heart heavier than ever in your chest. And then you've had enough of being alone.

You find Martin in the workshop behind the main greenhouse; he is rubbing linseed oil into the handle of an old rake. You can tell it's linseed oil from the thick putty smell of it.

'All it takes is a good sanding, and a couple of layers of oil,' he says, holding the rake out to admire. 'Fantastic old piece of beech.' He turns the rake upside down to inspect the metal prongs.

'And not a trace of rust left. See?' He looks at you directly, reads your face.

'Claire. What's wrong?'

You clench your jaw to stop your bottom lip wobbling.

'You were right about Evie,' you say, your voice hollow. 'She is not what I thought.'

You stand there looking at him, feeling the tears sting your eyes, slide down your face. You don't brush them away or try to hide. Martin does not look away. Instead he steps forward, opens his arms, holds you while you cry.

When you have cried enough, you stop. For long moments, you stay where you are, feeling his warmth against you. But you need to blow your nose. Without moving away, you say,

'My nose is running. I'm going to get a tissue. Don't look.'

You feel him smile against the side of your head. Then he steps back, makes a point of turning away.

'I'm not looking,' he says. 'Off you go then.'

—

35

In the seconds between sleep and waking, a door swings open. You see your father sitting next to your mother by her bed. The circle of light from the bedside lamp embraces them both.

———

As winter nears, you are developing a passion for lists.

This month, you will order seeds.

You will gather the last of the fallen leaves and burn them.

You will check that tree stakes are stable, the ties not cutting into the bark.

You will clip bubblewrap to the greenhouse frames for insulation; clean and trim the wicks on the paraffin heaters.

This month, you will soak cyclamen seeds, then sow them in trays of compost. You will keep them damp without water-logging them.

Sometimes, you remember it as though Evie rose up in her bed, hung over you like a malicious angel. You wonder what Margaret did after you left; whether she confronted Evie or kept the knowledge close to her chest, as Evie had done. You consider the stretch of days, the weeks since you were last there; imagine the house with the two of them in it, with the secret that is no longer a secret.

Next month, you will treat the timber of sheds and fences with preservative.

You will use bleach to clean moss and lichen from the paths.

You will tidy the storage areas at the nurscry; throw out broken pots and empty compost bags, etcetera.

In winter, morning sunshine increases the risk of frost damage; it thaws frozen plant tissues too quickly, rupturing the cell walls. You will protect tender trees and shrubs by packing straw around them.

———

36

Rain. You like it when rain is soft, when it settles gently, with respect. But now it's raining hard, in sheets, sounding like a machine on the roof, browbeating the lane and ferns and brambles. It gives you the same unsettled feeling you get from the sea, the feeling of things being stirred up.

When it stops, you open the kitchen door and stand just inside, breathing the clean washed air. Everything drips. Everything is scoured clean, bent over. The geraniums around the door have been flattened, their leaves are plastered with mud. But they'll be fine in a day or two, as good as new.

When the telephone rings, you expect Martin's voice, something to do with the nursery. But it is Margaret Keyes. She has some news, she says. She thought you should know.

Evie has died.

Evie's heart stopped early this morning.

'I went in to open her curtains. I didn't notice. I thought she was still asleep. When I went back with her lemon juice, I realized.'

Margaret's voice is tinny, as though some of it is getting stuck in the telephone line. You wonder what she is really feeling. You think about the hostility between them. The battle of wills, the spitefulness. How much worse did it get after you left? Disquiet raises the hairs on your arms. A thought begins to form, and a question. You cannot bear to think it; you turn elsewhere.

'What will you do now?' you ask.

A long time before she answers.

'I don't know. Every day, I've known exactly what to do, what time to do it. Until today. The doctor came. The ambulance came and took her away. I changed the sheets and made the bed.'

You say nothing. You hold the receiver next to your ear, your eyes on the rainspattered window; the largest raindrops are trickling down into other drops, making slow rivulets to the bottom of the pane.

'Could you come to her funeral?' Margaret asks. 'There will be no-one else there except me.'

No.

You should say no.

You say: 'I don't know, Margaret. Let me think about it.'

You park opposite the house, on the far side of the road, glad that Margaret has never seen your car and won't recognise it. You turn off the ignition, undo your seatbelt. From here, you have a view of the sea shining pale grey at the bottom of the avenue. The sun is warm through the windscreen, but when you roll down the window the air is cold enough to make you shiver; you roll it up again, leave a crack open at the top.

The house looks just the same. The red bricks glow in the late autumn light; the windows glitter.

You picture the wax-scented hallway. The sinuous banister, the quiet stairs. Evie's room, bed empty, the velvet bedspread smooth. You picture the dark shambles of the back garden.

The images slide by; you observe them. You had expected to feel something more.

There's an envelope on your mat. Lilac, the colour of hushed voices. For a moment, you wonder if it might be a sympathy card, but you haven't told anyone Evie is dead. You turn the envelope over and recognise your father's handwriting. It's a birthday card. Irises in a china vase and Best Wishes on your Special Day in pink italics. *Love from Dad* in black ballpoint, in writing that is almost printing, with only one or two letters joined up.

He never forgets. There is always a card, always on time. You have taken them for granted, these small reminders that he is still there, still in the background of your life.

> What will it be like, that first birthday I don't receive a card from my father?

There is every chance that the world will lurch on that day, tilt on its axis. You wonder how you will survive the bare mat. You put the card on the kitchen windowsill.

Making stew, you chop the carrots into rounds, precisely, like your mother would have done. There was a time when you would have done it differently, just to have done it differently from her. Now you scoop up the orange disks and drop them into the pot, seeing your mother's hands, her careful movements, in your own.

Before it gets dark, you go out into the garden to take photographs. The bark of the oak trees makes a pattern of cracks and ripples. It draws you in; you sink; you settle. There are spaces in it, tiny places that hold air and house small creatures, give purchase to plants. Close up, it looks like an aerial view of deserts and mountains.

At the bottom of the garden, you photograph the twisted roots of the ash. The stream is sluggish, the water gloomy and flat. Hard to believe it's the same stream, so busy with all kinds of small life in the summer. You wonder about the water skating insects, whether they are hibernating or have died. You have watched them for hours, their feet poking tiny dimples in the water, never breaking the surface. But you have never seen them tear the skin of the water and sink down into it.

———

37

The small chapel is nearly empty and there's too much light – light wood, light windows with bright abstract stained glass, white walls. It's not what you would have chosen for Evie. From the doorway you can see Margaret's back, wide and solid in black in the pew at the front on the right. She's wearing a hat, an almost brimless black felt hat. From behind, her head looks too small for her body.

There are six men in black suits at the back on the left. The pallbearers, the undertaker's men. Your footsteps clack down the aisle to the middle, where you slide into a pew on the left, aligning yourself with those who are there out of duty. Margaret turns round, nods, her face businesslike.

She could at least look a bit grateful.

But it's always hard to know what Margaret is feeling; she can make her face as blank as cardboard. You remember the thin sound of her voice on the phone when she told you Evie was dead; you have no idea what is in Margaret's mind and heart.

The air is full of soft anonymous classical music that Evie would have despised. And a surprising smell of cleanness, of citrus, light and pleasant. You settle into the pew, adjust to the hardness of the wood beneath you. Almost immediately, you feel the lethargy that descends on you in churches.

You look down at your knees, your feet, the wooden floor. At the green hymnbooks placed at intervals along the pew. At the ceiling above you, plain white. At the coffin, dark wood, resting on the plinth at the front.

There is no hint of Evie's presence in this place. You have to remind yourself: *Evie is in that coffin.* You imagine the small husk of her body, fragile, in peacock blue satin, her closed eyelids grey and impassive under the padded lid.

You wonder who washed her body for the last time. Would it have been Margaret? Margaret, who had washed her so often when she was alive, who had dealt with her mess and temper. You wonder what will be done with the ashes.

There are no hymns. Just the barest words – no attempt to express Evie's character. You imagine the priest talking to Margaret, asking for the personal details that would help him prepare the eulogy. *Did she have any hobbies or interests? What will people remember best about her?* You feel your lips move towards a smile. He didn't get what he needed from Margaret.

He should have asked you; you could have told him.

She found out where people were damaged and took advantage of them. She let her best friend get away with murdering her husband.

The priest is a stocky man with short grey hair. He has a nice voice.

'I am the resurrection and the life,' saith the Lord. 'He that believeth in me, though he were dead, yet shall he live.'

She encouraged people to trust her. She made a virtue of speaking her mind. You'd never have guessed she was a liar.

The Lord is my shepherd; I shall not want. He maketh me to lie down in green pastures; leadeth me beside the still waters.

She understood so much. With her words, her expressions, her silences.

She made a space in which I dared be myself.

Surely goodness and mercy shall follow me all the days of my life: and I will dwell in the house of the Lord forever.

I loved her.

I loved the person I thought she was.

You feel tears stinging your eyelids and you blink them back. Evie doesn't deserve your tears.

They are not for her.

The thought floods through you.

It's not Evie's betrayal that hurts so much. Not this much. You have been hurt this way before, used and left by someone you loved, someone infinitely more important than Evie. This is about you and your mother.

Still.

After all this time.

Our Father who art in heaven

You don't join in out loud but you can't help accompanying the words in your mind.

Forthineisthekingdomthepowerandtheglory.

As a child, you had resented this Father who owned everything, forever and ever amen, with no room for negotiation.

We therefore commit her body to the ground; earth to earth, ashes to ashes, dust to dust; in the sure and certain hope of the Resurrection to eternal life.

As he speaks, Evie's coffin sinks down into a recess in the floor. Your mother's coffin didn't do that. At your mother's funeral, there were heavy red curtains that closed around the coffin as Pachelbel's Canon surged through the audio system. It was unsatisfactory; you knew she was still there behind the curtains. What you really needed to know was that she had gone. That she was far away, too far to be able to reach you, and that was why you couldn't see her ghost. Not because she didn't care.

In the days after your mother died you spent a lot of time in your room. You said: *please come, let me see you, I can't be left like this*. You said it out loud. She didn't come.

It's over. Margaret Keyes is speaking to the priest. You stand up and leave the way you came in; it's even brighter outside. The circular car park next to the chapel is surrounded by tidy lawns, tidy gravestones, plaques of careful remembrance. You walk a slow circle along the edge of the tarmac.

In loving memory of Nigel David Slater 1962-2002
A wonderful Husband and Father

The stones are shiny black marble, the letters perfectly machined.

In memory of Rachel Louise Ballantyne 1936-2007
Gone, not forgotten

Your father took your mother's ashes with him. He might have scattered them somewhere special to the two of them, but you doubt it, can't imagine him letting them go. And the only place she would have wanted to be was with him. You imagine an urn of some kind, something beautiful, somewhere he can always see it.

Heavy footsteps behind you. Margaret. You don't want her to see you have been crying, don't want her to think your tears are for Evie. You needn't have worried; she looks anywhere but at your face.

'That's that, then,' she says, at last, her eyes on the ground.

Has she been crying too? It dawns on you that Margaret has just attended her own mother's funeral. That she sat through the service completely alone, knowing how much Evie had despised her.

You feel a twinge of sympathy for Margaret, a spasm that almost immediately transmutes into anger with Evie.

And if I feel this, how angry must Margaret have been?

You see:

Margaret's face swollen with rage, her big hands in fists. She stands over Evie's bed, unable to find the words. Evie looks straight into Margaret's eyes, smiles hatefully into her face.

A gust of wind rattles the fallen leaves in the car park. The disquiet you felt when you spoke to Margaret on the phone rises in you again. The question you have been avoiding crystallises. You open your mouth to ask. *Did you do it, Margaret? Did you kill her?* But the words won't come. You study her face for signs. There are none.

'Margaret.'

She looks up at you, squinting in the sunlight.

'I wanted to say – ' you cough, look away from her and back again. 'Just that I'm sorry. About what I said to you when I left that last time. I was so angry with Evie.'

She blinks, says nothing.

'It was wrong of me,' you go on. 'Blurting it out to you like that. I'm really sorry.'

She looks around, at the chapel, the lawns. You are not sure she is going to reply.

'I found a box,' she says at last. 'In her things. Files full of photographs and reports going back to when I was a child. She kept track of me for years.'

The wind gusts again; Margaret stuffs her hands into her coat pockets.

'Pages and pages of information. School reports. Even a copy of my son's medical report.' A current of anger ripples on the flat surface of her voice.

'How could she have got hold of that?' she asks, suddenly fierce.

You shake your head. You don't know.

'And there was a copy of the letter she wrote to me all those years ago. She wrote, you know, asking me to meet her.'

'Yes, I know.'

Margaret's eyes narrow. 'She used her maiden name. I would have known who she was if she hadn't changed her name. She bought the care home where my son stays. Did you know that? Seems you can do anything if you have enough money, enough time.' She turns to walk back to the black car that is waiting to take her home.

'What were your adoptive parents like?' you ask, walking next to her.

'They were fine. They made lots of mistakes. But the thing is,' she looks intently at you. 'They didn't owe me anything. They didn't *have* to give me a home or take care of me. They chose to. So even when they got it a bit wrong, I was grateful.'

She stops at the car, turns to you.

'It's helpful to think that way. About everyone, really.'

'Not Evie, though,' you say.

'No. Not Evie.'

Margaret is clumsy getting into the back of the car. She fumbles with the window, rolls it down.

'Thank you,' she says. 'Thanks for coming.'

You imagine holding this colour in the palm of your hand, rounded and smooth, the pale greenblue of a duck's egg. You love it just as much now as you did the day Martin brought it for you; it glows on the walls, even on dull days. And now there are new gauzy cream curtains, a cream carpet. There are soft scatter cushions on the leather sofa. And on one wall, there are framed botanical prints. *Passiflora violacea. Helleborus orientalis.* This room is yours now.

You sit cross-legged on the floor, your back against the sofa, the wooden box in front of you. You run your fingers over the mother of pearl on the lid, wondering who it was that cut all these small pieces and set them so carefully into the dark wood, hoping it was done with patience and satisfaction. You open the box and, one by one, spread your mother's letters out in front of you: twenty three envelopes arranged in a fan, like a spread of blank cards. You place your father's birthday card, the watercolour irises, below it.

You pick up your mug of tea, hold it between both hands, enjoying the warmth of it while you consider the envelopes. Today, you are not going to choose one at random in the usual way. Today, there is a particular letter you want to read, a letter that was in your mind when you woke up this morning. You cannot tell, looking at the envelopes in front of you, which one it is. You sip your tea.

Outside, it is raining gently. Nothing like the storming rain that preceded Margaret's phone call and the news of Evie's death. You replay the funeral like a film in your mind. As you reach the last scene – your conversation with Margaret outside the chapel – the film slows. A slow prickle of heat creeps up your neck. It is a feeling you have been warding off all day. Now you let it rise in you until you can name it.

Shame.

You are ashamed of your behaviour towards Margaret. You are ashamed that you sided so easily, so mindlessly, with Evie. Margaret Keyes is an easy target, slow and unappealing. You should have had more respect.

You hold the warm mug against your cheek, but the warmth is not a comfort. It turns out that Margaret is a more generous person than you have ever been.

'Even when they got it a bit wrong, I was grateful.'

You sigh, put your mug on the floor. Starting at the left, you pick up an envelope, open it, scan the page. You refold the letter, put it back in the envelope, back in the box. You find the one you want about half way through.

Dearest Claire,

Did I ever tell about the time, when you were six months old, that I nearly dropped you in the street? I was carrying you to the clinic for your check-up, and I tripped over the curb. I could feel myself tipping over, knowing I couldn't put my arms out to break my fall. I arrived at the clinic with blood dripping from my knees but you didn't have a scratch on you. They spent more time patching me up than checking you over. But you were a healthy baby, always hungry, very loud. We thought we had a future opera singer on our hands!

Your father used to get up to feed you in the nights, I bet you didn't know that. He was much better at making your bottle than I was, very sweet with you, even when he was tired. By the time you have children, I'm sure all husbands will be expected to help out, but it was quite unusual back then.

All my love.

You read the letter twice. Then you fold it away, put all the envelopes back in the box, close the lid. You pick up the card from your father.

Love from Dad.

———

38

The sea is the colour of slate, the sky only a few shades lighter. Evie would have loved it. From inside the car, you watch silent waves slap against the shingle, silent seagulls whirling over the spray. When you get out, the sound gusts over you: the waves, the seagulls, the wind. You are assaulted by it and by the cold. You pull the collar of your coat closed at the throat as you scuttle for cover.

The last time you came here, the apartment block was newer, brighter. Now the cladding on the balconies has faded and there are streaks of orange where the metal has rusted. The lift is noisy, a bit smelly. Instead of a mirror, there is a panel of shiny tin. You are reflected without detail.

In the moment before your father opens the door, you wonder if you will recognise him *the door will open and it will be a stranger standing there, someone you've never seen before* but of course you do recognise him, although you are shocked at how much older he looks. You want to tell him off for choosing the old cardigan and the corduroy trousers that make him look like an old man. His hair is still too long, still flops over his forehead. But it is almost entirely grey now.

'Claire.' He stands there, not knowing whether to hug you. He raises his hands, palms upwards, drops them again.

'Hello, Dad.'

'Come in, come in.' He steps back, makes room for you.

You stand at the window while he makes the tea. There is too much sky, too much water. On sunny days, the light would hurt your eyes.

'We get some astonishing sunsets here.'

He has popped back in from the kitchen, presumably while the kettle boils.

'Look. Fishing boats.' He hands you a pair of binoculars and ducks back into the kitchen while you obediently put the lenses up to your eyes, make out fuzzy grey sky. Or is it sea? You fiddle half-heartedly with the focus, put the binoculars back down on the windowsill, sink into one of the saggy armchairs. Books. Lots of books. He hasn't been able to resist starting a whole new collection – and there's a two-foot high pile of newspapers next to the fireplace.

You study the framed photographs on the mantelpiece. Your mother on their wedding day. You and your mother on a yellow blanket in the woods. He took that one – you can see the edge of his shadow intruding onto the blanket, reaching for her ankle.

'It's a shame there's no-one about,' she had said. We could have asked them to take one of all of us. We hardly have any pictures of us all together.' She wasn't unhappy, though. She blew a kiss through the lens to your father.

'Are you ready now?' you had whined. 'You said you'd come with me.'

'Do I have to, Claire? Can't you go collecting on your own for a little while?'

'You said you would.'

So she had. The two of you had combed the undergrowth for interesting shapes in wood and bark. Leaves, moss, seed pods. She found a small sharp rock that she said looked like a prehistoric tool, although you doubted it. You found a colony of small black ants in an old tree trunk. You peeled off a piece of bark and they scattered. You broke off a larger piece of the rotten wood, revealing shiny white eggs like tiny grains of rice. The ants picked them up in tender jaws, whisked them away into deeper crevices. When you looked up, your mother had disappeared. She and your father were lying on the yellow blanket, she with her head on his stomach.

'Oh there you are, darling,' she said, looking up, shading her eyes with one hand. 'I thought you would be there forever, watching those creepy crawlies.'

Your father was resting one hand on her shoulder, holding a curl of her hair between his thumb and fingers.

'You remember that day?' His voice is quiet behind you. You turn and take your mug of tea from him with unsteady hands.

'Not really,' you say. And then you see, in his eyes, how much he wants you to remember. That he needs to share the memory with you. Something dark twists in your stomach. Guilt. It's the least you can do, help him keep her memory alive.

'It was at Old Wood, wasn't it?' you say. 'We had a picnic for her birthday. No cake, she didn't like cake. But she ate a whole jar of olives.'

He smiles, grateful. You pretend to smile.

> I haven't been here five minutes and already he wants to talk about her.

> He hasn't even asked how I am.

'How are you?' he asks then.

'Fine.'

'Still working at the nursery?'

'Yes, still there. They might expand. Start a mushroom farm. Not for definite. Just an idea.'

'That's interesting,' he says.

But it's not, you know. Not to your father, who is only interested in words in books. In pages between covers. He's not interested in mushrooms, in your work at the nursery, not really. The two of you sip your tea. He breathes heavily through his nose, like he always did when he didn't know what to say to you when you were a child. He looks sad, and that makes you sad. More than you would have expected, it hurts to know that he is still unhappy, still lonely. And it's irritating too. You want to shake him.

Get over it, Dad. There's more to life.

He is looking out the window.
'Did you see the boats?' he asks. 'Through the binoculars?'
'Yes.'
'Oh, good.'
'Are they out there every day?'
'Not every day. Most days. It depends on the weather.'
'Oh. Of course.'
'Quite an uncertain livelihood, I should think,' he smiles, presses his lips with the tips of his fingers, breathes heavily through his nose again.

Something hurts somewhere between your chest and your stomach. You know you could stay here all afternoon, then leave, without ever really saying anything. Without being seen at all. Your father peers out the window, the old cardigan hanging from his narrow shoulders.

The ache in your chest gets worse; you can feel it pressing against your ribcage, at the notch in your collarbone, rising up into your throat. This is why you don't come and see your father. This feeling.

'Dad,' you say, and he looks round at you.

'I need to tell you something about Mum,' you say. 'About the night she died.'

He frowns, not at you, but at the word 'died' – he has always said 'since your mother left us' Never 'died.' As if 'died' is too strong a word.

'Remember her tablets,' you say, swallowing as the ache in your chest threatens to block your throat. 'The pink ones? I used to give her one every night so she could sleep.'

'Yes, of course.'

He is staring into space again.

'Dad.'

'What?' He brings you back into focus and seems to realize you are upset.

'What's wrong, Claire?'

'The tablets. I left the bottle of tablets by her bed. She distracted me and I forgot them. And then I remembered later, but I didn't do anything.'

You feel his hand on your arm, tentative. He has never known if it was alright to touch you, but now it helps. The words rush out of you.

'I left the tablets next to her and the next morning she was dead. She took the tablets, she planned it, she made me forget them and then she took them all and I hate her that she did that, Dad, I hate her, she planned it and left me alone, knowing – '

You need to take a breath now, but you can't. The feeling is swelling in your chest, your throat, you can't breathe around it, you try to say something else and all that comes out is a wail, a thin, narrow sound. And then you take a heaving breath and it turns into a sob and you are wailing, crying tears that feel as though they are concentrated, too strong, so salty it hurts to cry them. You hug yourself, hiding your head in the crook of your arm, your face wet and hot.

Your father's hand is still on your arm. You are aware of it, of his hesitant patting as you cry. Eventually, you rub your eyes on your sleeve, straighten up, wipe your hands over your face. Finally you look at him. He is frowning.

'Claire, let me be sure I understand you. You think your mother tricked you into leaving the sleeping tablets, then took them after you had gone to bed?'

You nod.

He takes you by the shoulders, looks you straight in the eyes.

'Claire. Listen to me. You had nothing to do with your mother's death. Nothing. I promise you that.'

There is absolute certainty in his voice. You study his face for signs of doubt. There are none.

'It was me,' he says.

For a moment, you don't understand what he means. He makes it completely clear.

'I gave her the tablets that night; I helped her take them. It was me.'

———

The pier is falling into disrepair; half of it has been closed down. There's a small amusement arcade, a fish and chip stall; the rest of the shops are boarded up. You buy one portion of chips to share between you, very hot, not quite cooked through, but the salt and vinegar taste good in the cold air. The wooden walkway is still open; you walk right to the end, lean against the iron railings together, buffeted by the wind. Your father scans the horizon but you watch the water below, churning against the thick pillars. It makes you dizzy; you shut your eyes. See:

> *A door swings open. Your father is sitting next to your mother by her bed; the pink pills are spread out on the bedside table. His chair is pulled close, his knees pressed into the side of the mattress. He leans forward, clasps one of her hands between both of his. He raises it to his face, rests his cheek in her open palm. Her eyes are dull and tired, sunk deep in the hollows of her face, but she watches him carefully.*

> *'Are you sure?' he says, and his voice is thick.*

> *She swallows with difficulty. 'I'm sorry.' Shuts her eyes, and tears slide easily from under her lids, over the sharp cheekbones, into the pillow.*

> *'Shh, shh, no. Don't be sorry, my darling. Never be sorry. You've been so brave, so brave.'*

The room is half dark; the one small lamp throws a circle of soft light. You watch as he feeds her the tablets, places them on her tongue one at a time, holds the glass of water as she swallows. When all the tablets are gone, he strokes her hair back from her forehead. Gently, so gently.

'Thank you,' she whispers.

He leans forward again, touches her forehead with his lips.

'Good night, my darling. God bless.'

———

'Will you come again?' he asks, flicking chips out over the water for the gulls. 'If you have time? I know it's a fair distance, but it would be good to see more of you.'

'Sure, Dad. Yes it would.'

You breathe in, call on all your senses, strip away the last layers between you and the moment. You want to remember it. All of it.

The taste of salt and vinegar.

The wind pushing in from the sea.

The gulls crying and cartwheeling over the waves.

The feeling, like new pink shell under your breastbone, of something changed.

And your father standing next to you.

———

You can't sleep. You kick off the duvet and get up. In your parent's bedroom, you take the folded bedspread from the shelf in the wardrobe, lay it on the bed, on top of the blue wool blanket. You stroke it flat, then sit in the middle of the bed, in the middle of the map that had defined things so clearly for you as a child.

The herringbone stripe is a railway track, the yellow one is a road.

The blue one is a river.

The room is chilly, you pull the bedspread up around your shoulders. It smells slightly musty, but mostly it smells of the dried lavender in the wardrobe. You wrap it close.

Things have changed.

I am not the girl who helped to kill her mother.

My mother is not the woman who tricked me into doing it.

My mother's last kiss was not a betrayal. It was a goodbye.

Your anger falls away like a cliff face into the sea.

You cry with your mouth open, until your eyes hurt and your face feels stuffed with tears.

And then you are tired. And then you sleep.

You are as close to the glass as you can get. Behind it, silver air bubbles spin to the surface like living creatures. Amongst them, fish with transparent bodies, with visible spines and bones, are coasting on the currents.

'This is it,' Martin had announced as he stopped the Land Rover in front of the sealife centre. He reached in front of you, into the glove compartment and held out a ticket.

'Your belated birthday present from me,' he grinned, and pressed it into your hand.

'Aren't you coming?'

'Absolutely not,' he said. 'Now go on, I'm on double yellow lines.'

You slipped off the seat down onto the pavement and watched as he drove off waving.

Inside, the Victorian building smells damp, like a tunnel. It's gloomy, the aquariums are shining windows in the walls. You take your time, enjoying the arch of the vaulted ceiling above you, the feel of the black and white tiles under your shoes. At each window, you stand close, forget the glass, take your awareness into the water, amongst the creatures there. There are flat pink fish with lazy fins, grazing the bed of their tank like a herd of tiny cows. Large rubber-skinned fish with yellow eyes. Skittish angelfish. Sleek grey fish cruising at speed like a hunting pack.

You find a window full of pufferfish and think of Matti. Maybe you will come back again and bring Matti with you, although the pufferfish are strangely deflated now, their spines lying flat like feathers.

There is a terrapin tank where an artificial waterfall falls constantly; you wonder whether the turtles find it irritating, the incessant vibration of the water as they hang there, snouts just above the surface; or whether it is reassuring to them. Perhaps it sounds like home.

There is an open lagoon of grey stingrays; they ripple and dive, flickering white underbellies. There is the walk-through tunnel, a glass corridor through the water; you press your face close as a shark barges through blue light. Then, in the last tank, there are seahorses. Fins fluttering, tails curled around the waterweed, they nod in the current. *A seahorse beats its fins* you read on the notice *as fast as a hummingbird's wings – seventy beats per second.* They have fierce little faces, like miniature dragons.

You have tea in the café at the centre of the aquarium. The tea is tepid, the chair uncomfortable; it doesn't matter at all. You are surrounded by windows of living fish. Healthy, happy fish in clean water. All in the right tanks, the vulnerable are separate and safe from the predators.

When you come out, Martin is leaning against a fibreglass sculpture of the Nautilus, waiting for you.

'Did you enjoy it?' he wants to know.

You tell him yes.

Your chest is a warm bright space inside you.

—

41

There is a letter. A plain white envelope with your address typed in bold behind the see-through window. It's not a bill, not junk mail. You turn it over in your hands, looking for a clue, then slice it open with a kitchen knife.

It's from a solicitor. You read it too quickly, scanning the page, catching pieces of the sentences. It says Mrs Eveline Bell has left you something in her Will.

You feel sick to your stomach, remembering the day you arrived to find Evie's solicitor with her, the man with the pink face and wispy hair. You remember how you waited downstairs, resenting the rumble of his voice, and the silence you shared with Margaret after he left.

Neither of you had said what you were both thinking: that Evie had changed her Will; that she had written you into it. And now it seems that was exactly what she had done.

The house. Your heart flips.

Could I really still want the house?

No. If she has left you the house – if for some perverted reason she has left you the house – you will never set foot there again. You will tell the solicitor to get rid of it; you don't want anything to do with it.

Then you re-read the letter properly and it says: *you have*

*been bequeathed an item from the estate of Mrs Eveline Bell…
please contact us to arrange to take possession of the item at
your convenience.*

So it isn't the house.

Whatever it is, you still don't want it.

—

The desk is massive, polished wood with swollen legs, the receptionist tiny behind it. She fixes you with calm grey eyes, confirms your appointment, asks you to wait.

You sit down and look around at the room, understated in muted colours, beige and cream with flashes of maroon. There is an oriental rug hanging on the wall near you, a small notice next to it, like in a gallery. *Persian Prayer Rug circa 1765.*

It's all very impressive, a stylish combination of the old and the new. But the chair you are sitting on is too upright, too hard. You shift on the seat, hoping the solicitor won't be long. Almost immediately, the lift bell rings and he is striding towards you, hand extended to shake yours. Today the shirt is pale yellow and he is not wearing a jacket. There is something unsettling about a man in a long sleeved shirt and tie without a jacket.

Like a turtle out of its shell.

He squeezes your hand in his own plump fist and ushers you into the lift. 'Thank you for coming, Miss Farrell,' he says, his voice deep and hearty. Too loud, really.

'It's Ms,' you say. He either doesn't hear or doesn't respond.

The lift is small, old fashioned. Pressed into a corner, you can clearly smell his aftershave, spicy and light. He keeps himself gathered in, arms by his sides, eyes on the lift buttons. Even so, he's too close; you're glad his office is only two floors up.

'In here,' he waves you ahead of him. After the impeccable reception area, this is a surprise. Cramped, cluttered with files, boxes, books. There's a narrow window, too high to see out of. A desk and a table, both overflowing. Two plain visitors' chairs.

You sit in one, fold your coat over the arm of the chair. He eases himself behind the desk.

'I won't keep you for long,' he says. He indicates a brown cardboard box on the desk.

'I'll just need you to sign for this.'

You sign your name in the space he points out to you; he slides the cardboard box over to your side of the desk.

'Thank you,' he says. 'And' – he passes you a clear plastic folder of papers – 'as a named beneficiary, you get a copy of the Will.'

Back in the lift, on your own this time, with the heavy box tucked under one arm. You glance at the folder before rolling it up to tuck in your bag, read the cover page through the transparent plastic:

In the Estate of Eveline Grace Bell (née Cullen) Deceased.

You set the box down on the bleached wood of the kitchen table. You take off your coat. You telephone Margaret.

'It's me,' you say, 'Claire.'

'Oh. Hello.' She doesn't sound surprised, or even interested, to hear your voice. But that's just Margaret.

'There's something I need to know,' you say.

'Hmm?'

'When Evie first wrote to you, asking you to meet her, what name did she use?'

Margaret doesn't even pause to ask why you want to know.

'Cullen,' she says. 'Her maiden name. When I met Eveline Bell, I didn't know she was the same person.'

'Thanks, Margaret,' you say, 'I have to go now.'

Your hand is shaking as you put down the phone.

You grab a thick jumper, pull it over your head, change your shoes for boots. You pick up a rake and a pair of gardening gloves from the store cupboard, the one that used to be the outside lavatory.

Working from one end of the hedge to the other, you rake the dead leaves out from underneath, exposing woodlice and glistening pink earthworms, leaving them stunned. The leaves are mostly from the sycamores in the lane. The hedge is beech and will hold onto its curled brown leaves throughout winter.

Evie is Grace Cullen.

Was.

You rake hard, scoring the damp earth. There are daffs planted under here. In two or three months they will send up green spears, although it's hard to imagine things not damp, not brown and cold.

It has stayed with you, that last glimpse of Evie alight with malice. So now when you picture her – whether the memory is of her laughing or listening or sharing her heart with you – you can't help but see the flicker of something dangerous just beneath the surface.

Grace Cullen.

The leaves are wet, they stick together in clumps, impale themselves on the rake. You have to stop and peel them off, can feel them cold and wet even through the thick canvas of your gloves.

Think. What did Evie say about Grace?

How close they were.
I knew her thoughts, often, before she spoke them.
That she was unkind.
Grace enjoyed cutting people with her words.
That she was demanding, extravagant, manipulative.
You had hated Grace almost from the start. Even before Evie told you that Grace had let Harold die.
She said she turned the radio up loud so she couldn't hear.

But that hadn't been Grace.

It was Evie.

You stop, stand leaning against the rake, breathing hard. The air tastes of wood smoke. You stand there until your breathing settles, until your blood stops racing, until the world is still and quiet. You start back at the other end of the hedge, rake the leaves together into a pile.

———

There is nothing comfortable about a stony beach in winter. The stones are so cold they feel wet, although you are well above the tide line. The sea slides in slowly and out again, as though it is less fluid, thicker, in the cold.

You crouch, settling your boots solidly onto the pebbles, feeling the muscles bunch in your thighs. You put Evie's final gift down on the stones. A couple walks past on the promenade above the beach; their voices carry in snatches on the wind.

That night, after you raked the leaves, you sat at the kitchen table with the cardboard box in front of you. You picked it up, tested its weight, put it down again. What was so important that Evie had changed her Will?

Whatever it is, it can't hurt me. She can't hurt me now.

But still, you had waited until after supper. Until after you had a bath and put on your pyjamas. Until you had brushed your teeth.

Then you peeled back the corner of the tape with your thumbnail and stripped it away, folded back the flaps of cardboard. You lifted out the tissue-wrapped object, peeled off the tissue paper, revealed the purple and gold pattern of Evie's hexagonal papier maché box.

Now you pull your scarf tighter and higher round your neck, trying to keep the cold out of your ears. You use your teeth to pull off one glove by its middle finger and remove the hexagonal lid.

Now, eyes narrowed against the wind, you picture Evie's face, bright and animated, when she first showed it to you: her collection of pebbles. You hear her voice: *They were a kind of treasure to me.*

Taking them out, one by one, you notice how much warmer they are than the stones on the beach. There is the smooth grey pebble seamed with white. The shiny black one. The oval red one with chips of orange. You take them all out, gathering them in a loose pile next to the purple box.

What do you think happened, Claire? Did these stones simply lose their value, locked away in this box for so long? Did it just drain out of them?

The clamour of the gulls is ragged on the wind; you look up and out across the sea. There is no clear horizon. Where they meet, the water and the air are the same shade of grey.

Once, with your mother, you saw snow falling into the sea. The fluffy flakes descended slowly, covering the beach in a thick layer, uneven at the waterline where the waves took bites from it. The air was full of white snowflakes that disappeared the instant they landed in the dark swelling water.

Your mother had squeezed your hand, the wool of her glove and your mitten together making a warm padding in your palm. She said: *remember this, the snow falling into the sea, it's magic.*

A circle of warmth opens up in your chest. The warmth expands, includes the memory of your father sitting on your mother's bed. You still can't quite take it in, that somehow he had found the strength to help her leave him. You are still adjusting to the new lightness within you, the absence of weight. You breathe in deeply, tasting the salt and the cold in the air, breathe out.

Your bare hand has gone numb with cold, you pull the glove back on, fold your fingers up and blow warm air into the middle of your fist. You pick up one of the stones, plain grey, smooth. It is a comfortable round shape in your palm.

Grace said they never did have any value. That I made them special, and I made them ordinary again.

You replace the grey stone, shift your weight; the pebbles of the beach grind under your boots.

You wonder how Margaret is adjusting to life after Evie, to her inheritance. That had been another surprise. After opening the box, you had looked at the Will more closely, turning the crisp white pages.

This is the last Will and Testament of me Eveline Grace Bell.

You had never seen a Will before; it was shorter than you expected, just three and a half pages, most of it dealing with the appointment and powers of her Trustees the solicitors. There was a sentence leaving you the box of pebbles. Then there was a sentence dealing with everything else.

I Give Devise and Bequeath all my remaining property both real and personal to Margaret Rosalind Keyes.

You had to read it twice more before you were certain you understood it correctly. Evie. Doing the unexpected. Delighting in her own perverse logic. You are certain she didn't do it out of the kindness of her heart.

Be that as it may, Margaret is a wealthy woman now. She will never need worry about her son's care again. You wonder what she will do.

She can get a kitten now.

It's a small thought, and silly, but you like it.

You had almost missed the rest. You almost put the Will to one side, thinking about Margaret's middle name, Rosalind, that it was unexpected, pretty. But you glanced at the bottom of the last page.

Signed by the above named Eveline Grace Bell.

And there was the signature: EGBell. The handwriting sharp, forward slanting, but clear. Evie had signed her name.

A gust of wind catches the hexagonal lid. It rolls a few feet across the beach, rattling over the stones; gets caught in a tangle of seaweed and old fishing line, shines there.

Even now, on the cold beach in the wind, you can sense Nanny Bee's handprint over your heart. It has occurred to you that she might always be close, whether you see her or not.

Of course you have wondered, have not been able to help it: *why not your mother's ghost? Where was she?*

There may always be things I don't know. Pieces missing.

You look for a tissue in your pocket; there isn't one. You wipe your nose on the back of your glove.

I made people take their own stones home with them. In fact, I made each of them feel it was a gift. They were grateful.

You narrow your eyes against the wind, feeling it scrape past your cheeks, hearing the hollow cold sound of it.

It's time to go.

You shut your eyes. All it takes is a gentle swipe to spread Evie's stones amongst the other pebbles on the beach. You hear them clatter and rub, then there is just the uneven sound of the waves. You open your eyes and stand up, feeling the blood rush into the backs of your knees.

And here we are

You turn and walk away, back up the stony beach.

You in my shoes; me watching still.

You climb the steps onto the promenade;

Thank you

Your footsteps are muffled on the concrete.

For your gift of looking closely.

The turquoise railing shines against the grey sky.

Thank you

For staying to the end.

Slip off my shoes, now
I am Claire.

About this book

This is a self-published novel, which means there isn't a global marketing machine behind it, just me. So if you enjoyed *The Gift of Looking Closely*, please recommend it by word of mouth or by writing an honest review about it on Amazon or any other website, or in your own blog or publication.

If you'd like to give me feedback, please visit my website www.albrookes.co.uk or send an email to al@albrookes.co.uk

I'd be delighted to hear from you.

~ *Al Brookes*

CPSIA information can be obtained at www.ICGtesting.com
Printed in the USA
LVOW07s1942240915

455582LV00007B/655/P